RIPFOLDS I

OPEN WOUNDS IN TIME

By: Robert A Wehrmeyer

ripfolds

In early 2005 a Cincinnati, Ohio based technology company was engaged by the Department of Defense to develop a viral based vaccine to help treat post-traumatic stress disorder and other divergent issues. A computer-generated virus was created and driven by the emotion of the host to attack memory. The virus went AWOL, mutated, spread outside of the intended scope and outside the company. All members of the science team were infected, all offspring of the science team thought to be carriers. Two of these progenies, Brandon Fair, the only son of the company's chief scientist and Julia Childs are infected but also very gifted.

This story is about three young teenagers: two with unique gifts to travel in time and one just unique. Brandon, Jules, and Jimmy learn early in life to think for themselves and care for each other.

"Ripfolds are like cuts or wounds in the sky," Brandon says to Jimmy. "Jules and I see the Ripfolds and know what they represent. When either Jules or I grab a fold, we are thrown into another place and time, inside another person. Once inside we are programmed to connect the person's memory to the lost moment and overcome the effects of the virus. If we don't connect the memory the Ripfolds will close and vanish. The virus is successful, and time is changed forever."

ISBN-13: 978-0-9845346-4-7

LCCN: 202591158

To order additional copies of this book, please go to:

www.ripfolds.com

Sue Toth, Editor

ACKNOWLEDEGMENTS

Lady Gaga, © Ate My Heart Inc., HP, © Hewlett-Packard Development Company L.P., Google, © Google LLC, Hemingway, © Hemingway Ltd., James Bond, © Danjaq LLC, University of Dayton, © University of Dayton, YMCA, © YMCA , Star Trek, © Paramount Global , Rolex, Daytona, © Rolex SA & Hans Wilsdork Foundation, Paul Newman, © No Limit LLC, Frisch's Big Boy, © Big Boy Restaurant Group, Pizza Hut, © Pizza Hut Inc., Wall Street Journal, WSJ, © Dow Jones & Company, Inc., Wendy's, © The Wendy's Company, Motorhead, © The 2015 Kilmister Trust, Lexus, © Toyota, IHOP, © Dine Brands Global, Inc., P&G, Procter & Gamble, © The Procter & Gamble Company, The University of Cincinnati, © The University of Cincinnati, Big Ten, © The Big Ten Conference, Inc., McDonalds, © McDonalds Corporation, Derrick and Dominoes, Domino's, © Domino's Pizza, Inc, Dayton at Wright Patterson Air Force Base, © U.S. Department of the Air Force, Hotel California, © Red Cloud Music and Cass County Music, Motown, © Universal Music Group, Dickens, © The Charles Dickens Estate, Poe, © Creative Characters, Inc., NBA, © NBA Properties, Inc., Metallica, © Metallica, West Point, © The United States Military Academy at West Point, Coke, Diet Coke, © The Coca-Cola Company, Spurs, © Spurs Sports & Entertainment, Cincinnati Zoo, © the Zoological Society of Cincinnati, Ray Bradbury, *Something Wicked this Way Comes,* © The Estate of Ray Bradbury, Whataburger, © BDT & MSD Partners, Futurama, © Disney, Department of Health, DOH, © the U.S. Department of Health and Human Services, Department of Defense, DOD, © The U.S. Department of Defense, Hallmark, © Hallmark Cards, Inc., Cadillac, General Motors, © General Motors, Hitchcock, © The Hitchcock Estate, Sherlock Holmes, © The Conan Doyle Estate, Obi-Wan Kenobi, © Lucas Film, Richard Hannah, *The Thirty-Nine Steps*, © John Buchan, Men In Black, © Columbia Pictures Industries, Inc., Miami Vice, © Universal Television, Universal Pictures, NBCUniversal Comcast, Snoop Dogg, © Calvin Broadus

Cover art and design for the Ripfolds series by, "An."

Cover photo by iStock.com /Adon Buckley/Canyon Iceland Aerial

DEDICATION, HISTORY AND BACKGROUND

To the "Teacher of English" (thank you, Tim) I met just a few short months ago who started me on the path to Ripfolds, I pray she is also writing her own dedication. Mostly to my mom, Pat and older brother, Mike, who both recently left this world. My mom, the loving warrior, hope God plays tennis. My two sisters, Linda and Jenny, proving daily the best of her lives on. Mike, in viral isolation, created a lifetime of artwork while cutting short his own.

Special thanks to Trey, Ashley, Frank Town and Steven Wehrmeyer. The youngest minds are often the brightest.

During the COVID crises and shut down, there was one scene that seemed to play out nightly. They ruled various media networks; families sitting, standing, laughing, and crying, attempting to communicate through a pane of glass. Mom, Dad, grandpa, or nana on one side and everyone else piled on the other. Each of us, in our own way, in our own nursing home, held captive by an invisible virus. Upward of two years of unrealized memories lost forever, lost to isolation and fear. _Sealed wounds in time_ never to be realized or performed. Never to unfold. Even history won't know what was lost, only gained. This story is about the Gains!

Two brief videos of my brother's artwork, the bulk of which was created during 2020-2021 COVID lockdown, can be seen on the website: www.ripfolds.com. We gained the artwork but lost the man.

This is a work -of- fiction. Any similarity to actual persons, living or dead or actual event is purely coincidental.

Excerpt from Ripfolds III, *In the Beginning*.

"John, I don't think you understand," Binky says one week after her success with the ball lightning experiment now sitting in John Alcott's office a part of her regular download to the Girta, President and CEO. "The ball lightning electroporation process allows the microbe to travel electromagnetically. The virus is transformed into a wave, a vibration but does not lose its programming. The pathogen is free to travel through space and time, and its only mission is to fulfill the application we planted. "What's that mean in dollars and cents," Alcott's terse response. "We need additional funding, or that Binky virus of yours won't be traveling on Southwest airlines," he barks back.

"John we turned living matter into light, and I think it still works. I don't want to be melo-dramatic, but we may have created a kind of time warp or worm hole, if you will. A way real matter can seamlessly travel in space and time and be targeted to perform a function. Alcott now, silent, it's sinking in, he gets it, he really gets it. After a time, his inside feeling a little like Edvard Munch's infamous "Scream," painting.

They both sit there clearly lost in their own thoughts. Minutes later Alcott mumbles, "this could be the most powerful weapon the world has ever seen." Binky off in her own world processing the next steps with her viral wave experiments. "What was that John?' she asks. "Nothing, nothing at all," he responds but then immediately commands, "get this written up pronto. Get me something to show those brainless bureaucrats at the base, now!"

Contents

PART I

OPEN WOUNDS IN TIME

Chapter One

A couple of months ago, I started seeing cuts or cracks in the sky. At first, I thought maybe it was a scratch or dust in my eye. When I rubbed my eyes, it was still there, at least for a moment. These things, these jagged cuts or tears appeared at various times, different locations, around town. They come and go fast and don't seem to last long. I don't see them that often, just from time to time. No real link to anything that made sense to me; at the crosswalk, the wall of the grocery store, stands at the soccer field.

These cuts were more like freshly cracked ice, splintered ice with little arteries shooting off in various directions. Each of these cuts or tears are unique but still basically the same. I have seen enough of them now, like long stretched holes in the earth and sky. Some are smaller or brighter than others. I have no idea why they might all be slightly different but still basically look the same--no, idea, no clue.

At this point I have seen enough of these cuts I think they are real. At least I believe these cuts or rips are real. For some reason, I want to believe they are real. I know you can reach out and touch or feel them. The rips have an energy, a light. The first time I came up with the courage to reach out to one, there was shock or jolt. It didn't hurt, no pain but powerful, and it pulled away even before I was upon it. And then it was gone, just vanished like the others. Like I said when I see them, they don't last long, they just come and go. At this point the disappearance doesn't really concern me, I know there will be others. I've come to believe there would be more. As I said they appear from time to time in various positions and places.

Of course, there is another alternative to the rips' or cracks' existence. I might not be all there, I might need help, might be missing a screw or two. At sixteen, it's not that hard to believe. Yes,

I believe I am normal, look and act normal, like girls, play basketball, eat a lot, don't drive yet so I tend to walk everywhere. I outgrew my bike a couple years ago.

A couple of days later now walking to the gym. I have basketball practice in two hours. I round the corner, and my right hand reaches up to catch the old light post.

Same light post I grab almost every day on the way to school. I use this post to swing around to face traffic just for fun. Just for something different and it makes me feel good. This time when I do it and about halfway around, there it is right in front of me, a rip, a tear. I reach out without really thinking, put my hand inside and bang, I am gone.

Dazed for a second or two, I find myself in the middle of what looks and feels like a car crash, a bad car crash, total mayhem.

"Holy shit," I scream out loud, crash, boom, bang, screaming, crying, sirens. The weird part, from what I can tell we are sitting in the front seat of a car smashed into the side of another car. We can't see much; there are other cars involved. We, yes, I said we. Next to me in the driver's seat is an old lady. There is the old light post, my personal swing. The post is through the windshield over the steering wheel and all the way through her, dead as a doornail. Even weirder, I see myself in the rearview mirror and I look like her, I am her, she's dead and I am her. I feel like me and I look like her, like I said—holy shit! Then I realize I never let go, never let go of the light post. My right hand is still holding onto the pole back in my world. I panic, struggle, yank then pull and find myself back to where I started out of the cut or rip. of car crash, no dead lady, no screaming or crying.

Just me again now swinging around the lamp post and back to where I started, like a hundred times before, a full three-sixty.

Time out, I am screaming to myself as my momentum brings me to a quick stop. I step aside and now frantically feeling my arms and legs, pull out my phone, fumble around for the camera, and hit reverse. I look like me, ragged out a bit but me, not some old dead lady, that's a relief. Now feeling around my body parts with more focus; face, arms, legs, all there. I then check all my parts and functions; best I can tell I am all there, all in one piece." Thank the Lord," I say out loud to only myself.

It's sunny, but not warm for November. Everything and everyone are going about their day. There's nothing out of the ordinary, no mayhem, no car crash, no crying, no dead bodies. Still sitting on the curb thirty minutes later, I once again reverse the camera on my phone, click a photo of myself just to make sure all is good. Everything is normal, as far as I can tell, everything in good working order. The home page lights up and I realize the time, now realizing I forgot about practice. Basketball practice starts in thirty minutes so quickly I get to my feet. "Thank God for basketball," I say out loud now starting to run.

Later that same day at home lying in bed now what, thinking to myself then say out loud, "not doing that again." Are you kidding me? Of course I am not doing that again, but I know at the time I am thinking and saying this I will do that again. I will try to do that again, in fairly short order and in some respect I know I have to do that again. Was that real or imagined? If these tears or rips don't turn out to be real, then I am probably crazy. I don't want to be crazy. I need to prove to myself that I am not. Also, I need to figure out why I get to be the lucky one? Why do I see these things when none of my friends seem to know anything about them? I've never mentioned anything like it, not found anything like this on the internet or part of any gaming I do. Not heard them mentioned in any media, reported anywhere as unusual or strange like, UFOs, Bigfoot, or Lady Gaga. Here I am just an ordinary, normal sixteen-year-old, growing pains, girl troubles, cranky parents, that's me.

I'm tall and lanky. My universe is fairly small: hoops; internet games, couple of friends, a dad and stepmom. My real mom passed years ago, and I have no brothers or sisters. I'm hoping to add

Alexandra to my personal loop, but I don't think she likes me yet. That's a problem.

Monday afternoon in early November after school and I'm walking to an early practice with my teammates and friends, trying to bring conversation around to the rips and cuts. My eyes have been playing tricks on me, I said to them, trying to draw them into a discussion. I wanted to see what they might know, if anything, about these mangled or twisted rips and tears in the sky. I told them, lately, occasionally, not very often I see a bright light like a line and hole in the sky.

"I rub my eyes and sometimes it's still there, now it's happening more and more kind of look like wrinkles or tears in the sky," I say. Nothing, no comments, no remarks, stone cold, they didn't take the bait. Then Jimmy says I might be going blind; I should stop playing with it or I will go blind soon. Everyone laughs. Jimmy is my best friend, but he can be a pain in the butt sometimes. Conversation then quickly disappears as we step up to enter the gym.

Later at home, I want to believe I am a normal teenager, have a normal teen schedule; school, basketball practice, eat and out with friends. Basketball is my thing. It comes naturally to me, and I am good at it. My friends call me Branded as in, "branded to be a star." Whatever, my real name is Brandon Fair. Ron, my dad, is fond of saying I have my, "mom's jet-black hair and his cold blue eyes." Maybe I am not so normal, I am thinking now, having done some research online but found nothing. Nothing to help one way or the other, good or bad. I've found absolutely nothing even remotely, related to these tears or rips. However, I am ready to learn more, maybe even ready to reach out and grab one. Just to see what happens. I need to see if they are real or imagined? Why they appear to me but apparently not to my friends or others?

So, here's the thing, it's a few weeks later, a few weeks after my car crashing roller coaster ride. For, now I am trying to think ahead if I try again, if they are real how can I enter one and still get back to the "here and now?"

How do I keep one foot in and one foot out? Since I don't really know how these things work, I have no idea what might happen. Just like the last time I needed to keep one hand on the pole. To do this I am thinking I need a tracker, yes tracker or footprint, maybe an online tracker or footprint. When I was in the rip, when I was the dead lady, in the middle of the car crash, it did not look like a long time ago or even futuristic. It looked a little like today. I probably have Internet, emails, and texts. So, I am thinking I need to keep connected maybe on the dark web whatever the heck the dark web is, because I have no clue, no idea. I need a virtual pole to hold onto if I get lost in the other world online. I can leave footprints and messages to help guide me along the way. As I mentioned, I am nothing special just an average, anxious, budding teenager thinking to myself now what could possibly go wrong.

It's the weekend, no school, no practice, and I have some free time so decide to take another look. I decided to take the long way around to the original crash corner, but I have not been there since the main event just a few short weeks ago. As I approach the corner, turn the corner really, the rip materializes. It's smaller, the cut is clearly smaller than it was, now just large enough for my one hand. What happened, I think to myself? It's clearly faded and smaller, the glow is much dimmer like it's vanishing, going away.

The next day, Sunday, I decided the best way for me to rejoin the rip world is to retrace my steps just like before. Same day of the week, same time, same clothes, same everything ready to try again, although I have avoided the same path to school since the first journey. This time I am careful to retrace my steps, the original path of course. I had no idea if the tear or rip will be there, if it will materialize. I can't make them appear or go away, they just show up. So just like a hundred times before, I am headed to the school gym the same way I used to take every day, just not lately. Coming around the bend, I can see the pole, the same pole as before, the same pole that can penetrate right through metal and other stuff. I reach up, grab with one hand, and start the swing about a third of the away around. Sure enough, there it is, like I said, much smaller, not as bright as if someone dimmed the light, shoved the corners together. But no matter, I reach out with my free hand and pierce the crack, Bang, I am gone, just like before.

This time I am sitting in the same car, no hand on the pole, now things are very different. I am still the dead lady, Maude, I am later to learn. But now I am sitting in the driver's seat, both hands firmly on the wheel.

Looking like a healthy Maude, probably just before the crash, I am guessing just before the crash. She, meaning we, are trying to leave the crash scene but can't seem to, the car is rocking slightly back and forth, back and forth not in a hurry like trying to escape the crash scene more like she must go somewhere, like just before the crash, she remembered she had to do something. My face, her face looks like we forgot to do something, looking very concerned or worried. She and I are trying to back out, still mayhem, still lots of cars, still lots of crushed, broken stuff including Maude and her car. The pole is down but all the crash stuff is now in front of us then something clicks inside Maude, I sense it. Maude and I are backing out like nothing happened with me driving. The car now works. Maude is no longer stuck in reverse. We can now go in reverse. I don't even have a driver's license yet, but with me driving we can go in reverse. Back to where we came from, we are clearly going back to where we started before the crash. A normal, clean four-door white sedan going back to where we started, old Maude and me at the wheel out for a friendly drive in the neighborhood.

I know now we are headed to Maude's house. I know this because I am her and can feel what she is thinking. She has to go back, she has to do something, something very important to her, something she forgot to do before she left this morning. We are headed to her house; we are not in a hurry, she knows where she is going. We are just cruising down the street, but I know where we are going and how to get there. We are going to her house to see her son, Johnny, who is at home in bed. Johnny is drifting, a loser by most accounts, but she loves him, he is her loser. He is lazy, doesn't work, not in school, no girlfriend, doesn't help around the house. However, Maude is thinking he needs to take his test today. She forgot to look in on him before she left, wake him up. It's important to me and Maude that Johnny wake up and take the test. She knows, we know his future likely depends on it. She has a good feeling about this test, she believes Johnny is going to do well. We can both sense it is time for him to move on.

Not ten minutes later we pull into our driveway single story, yellow brick house, small yard, grass, and hedges too long, little dirty and unkept--like Johnny. In park now, out of the sedan and grabbing the mail, mostly bills and junk. First envelope; Maude Simpleton, 111 Pinewood Drive, Sharonville, Ohio. I say this to myself once or twice until it hits me…Sharonville, that's where I live, that's here, in my world. Maude Simpleton lives in Sharonville, Ohio, like me. I don't recognize a thing, nothing looks familiar but why would it? I don't drive, and don't get out much, might live just over the hill for all I know. Well, this stink. I risk my life to jump into another world, another time and end up in my hometown. What happened to Paris, London, or even Columbus? Columbus, Ohio would be a giant leap over Sharonville!

We keep moving up the driveway now and into the house. As we walk in, Maude sits her keys down and yells, "Johnny I'm home." Maude lays the mail down on the desk in the hall on the way to his room. There is a computer on the table with an HP logo on the side of the machine, whatever that is? I think it's a computer. I wonder what an HP is, if it has internet or even email? Now we are in the bedroom and bending over Johnny, lightly shaking him, about to kiss his cheek. Seriously, I got to kiss this guy's cheek? Johnny, I say to myself inside Maude, "wake up its mom, time to get a move on, get showered, changed, and over to City Hall. They won't wait for you, must be on time, wake up," I say with a hearty shake to his shoulder. Then his eyes open, unfocused, and he begins to move.

Bang, almost as soon as Johnny shakes a muscle, I am back, back on the pole, swinging around the pole, but my head is swimming, nothing is clear, and I go flying hard into the sidewalk. I look up, groggy, totally discombobulated, knee is bleeding and sore, head hurts. A couple of little kids passing by, "What a dork" one says, and they all laugh. Maude is gone and it's just me, back to where I started.

As before, I just sit there for a while, a lot to take in and think about. What's next, I am thinking, what to do now, but realize while I am sitting there on the sidewalk, I know what to do, know my next move. I know the address where Maude and Johnny Simpleton live. As I scramble to my feet, surely looking a little frantic, disheveled, "I know her full name and address," I say out loud to no one in particular, "got to find a library, where the heck is the closest library?" I've never been in a library except the little bookstore they call a library at school. Do we have a library in Sharonville? They got to have one in Cincinnati. Cincinnati is huge, "Wait," I say out loud again, "don't need a library, I got Google."

I found a park bench and sit. It's getting cold, of course it's getting cold its almost Thanksgiving, Google: Maude Simpleton, 111 Pinewood Drive, Sharonville, Ohio, and up pops a picture of Maude, looking young, healthy, and smiling, the smiling picture attached to her obituary.

Dam this is freaky, this whole rip thing is freaking me out. A couple of paragraphs, short and sweet her entire life summarized in just a few sentences. The article refers to a traffic accident on November 17, 2007. The accident appeared to be caused by a series of mishaps; one of the cars run the light and hit a light pole. Four people dead, as many injured. Maude was forty-seven at the time, leaving an only son, Johnny, eighteen, and no other family. Many lives changed in the blink of an eye, including Maude's, Johnny's, and mine.

Google again, now I have Maude's full name, home address and the day she died. She died the day after tomorrow but ten years ago, today. She died on November 17, 2007. In two days it will be November 17, 2017. This time I click the headline from Google to the daily news concerning the accident ten years ago. Sure, enough it pops up, here it is, the whole story, the whole shebang. All the details about the accident, except, of course, no mention of Maude and me leaving the crash scene, leaving to go back to the house and wake up Johnny.

Two days later Its November 17, 2017. I decided to walk over to the pole, the scene of the accident and the scene of my first rip journey. Today is the day Maude died only ten years later and the day my life changed. No rip or cut in site, I sense now gone forever. As I approach, I see there is a policeman at the pole at the old accident scene. He is on one knee at the base of the old light pole, maybe still investigating the accident over ten years later like they do on COLD Files, the TV show. Then he gets up, hesitates for a minute, looks around, straightens up, brushes the dirt off his pant knee, puts his hat on and walks off.

He left something on the ground. I can see it as I walk slowly over to the pole. It's a flower, a red rose with a long thorny stem. I bend over and carefully pick up the flower. There is a little card, I hadn't noticed the card before now dangling, hanging by a thread. It's got painted hearts on one side. I flip it over, handwritten in blue pen, I read it aloud, "Miss you Mom, Love Johnny."

Chapter Two

"The major task of a linker is to search and locate referenced codes in a program and to determine the memory location where these codes will be loaded."

She jumped in ahead of me, stepped right in front of me, like I wasn't even there. Who or what was that? Where did she come from? I have seen many rips and tears now in numerous different places in and around town, but never another person, never another human, at least I assume human. A young girl about my age who obviously knows the rips, she obviously knows and sees what I see. Are there others who see and know the cracks and rips, I wonder? She didn't hesitate, jumped right in with obvious confidence, seemingly knowing what to expect, exactly what to do. Now what?

I don't remember much about my real mom. She died when I was young. She was Indian or as my dad says, Sikh. Sikh or Sikhism is a religion originated in the Punjab region of the Indian subcontinent Punjab, on the northwest corner of India close to Pakistan. I looked that up, guess that makes me half Sikh. I'm not sure you can be half a religion. Sikhs as a religious group are very disciplined, very committed, and not supposed to marry outside of the order. All the practicing males and females typically take the common last name, men, Singh (means Lion) and the woman, Kaur (meaning princess). My real mom was a rebel; she married my dad and took his surname. My dad is of English descent but has lived in the US of A all his life. Probably doesn't get much worse than that for a Sikh.

The British Crown ruled India for quite a while. Her name was Vinder Fair, a scientist and computer nerd, but everyone just called her Binky, including me, well, I was only six. All I really know now is she was her company's chief engineer and a computer whiz.

Binky was called a Bio-scientist, according to my dad, also one of the first "real" computer program developers, also according to my dad. I know she worked for a local Evandale company owned by an Indian couple. The company specialized in highly sensitive development work for the Federal Government. After she died, dad would talk about her work and the Girta Technologies Company, typically, when we were sitting around watching TV or at dinner. It meant nothing to me, but now I wish I had listened closer. After mom was gone, he would just start rambling about Sikhs, Mom, and Girta. Every now and then he would go into auto pilot and his "go to" was always the same; "Sikhs know service, nobody knows service like the Sikhs." He meant it I could tell, to a Sikh, Life is Service, Service is Life, he would say. I have no idea what that really, means, especially to my dad.

It's a week before Thanksgiving and basketball season is starting. We are well into pre-season conditioning and practice. I am a sophomore but playing varsity. I was on the varsity squad last year but didn't play much. My friends all thought I should have started, but the coach is a little sensitive about the freshman thing. In any event he can't stop me this year, I am clearly the best player on the team. We have our first scrimmage today, and I'm now on the high school bus trying to keep my mind on basketball. Truth be told, I don't think about basketball much these days. I don't think about Alexandra much either, who needs a girlfriend anyway? Let's face it it's not easy to concentrate on high school stuff when you have been through a virtual sex change with the dead, now, of course, thinking of Maude.

Today we play the second game of a Saturday afternoon pre-season tournament. Eight teams are involved. We play Cincinnati Moeller, a bunch of tough Catholic kids. We are the Sycamore Aviators. Most of my teammates are from in and around Sharonville. As we entered, I can hear and now see the gym is crowded for an early season tournament while the Reading Blue Devils are playing the Loveland Tigers. We play next. As we stroll in, I can see our JV coach on the other side of the court waving us over to the far side of the stands. We are bunched up at the entrance but at the first break in the action we all head over. As we turn the corner to the Loveland side, I spot her, there she is. I do a double take then look again. It's her, I know it's her, the rip girl, the, "jump right in" girl and she is staring right at me. Our eyes locked and I quickly look away toward the floor, noticing the game had started again. I quickly look back over my shoulder. She is still staring right at me, so intense then I run right into the back of Jimmy, pushing him slightly onto the floor. The coach sees this, thinks we are goofing, and screams at us from the corner of the gym. Jimmy was just laughing. Nothing upsets Jimmy, but when I recover and look back up to the stands, nothing. I look around frantically and nothing, she is gone.

Later that night I am thinking, she was on the Loveland side, she is a Tiger. Not sure how to track her down, but it doesn't take me long to find out a few Loveland after school hangouts. From my choices I decide to focus on the Study Place, the most popular. I decided also to leave a somewhat anonymous note on a local online chat room for area high schoolers. No way of knowing if she looks at these or ever goes to the Study Place, but what the heck, many of the Loveland students do, what do I have to lose? The Study Place is in a small strip center just a few blocks from Loveland high school, has pizza, brew pub, couple of empty shop areas and the Study Place. The Study Place is set up for kids to get together and study. The shop sells coffee on one side, donuts to the other and who knows what else after dark? It's open late every night except Sunday.

As I mentioned, I don't drive yet, so I walk over to the Study Place and take a table. It's Friday afternoon about a week after the scrimmage game where I saw her. We have the day off because our first real game, our first season game is Tuesday night. After an hour of sitting there, my head on a swivel, the coffee and suspense get to me, and I must pee. As I stand over the stall relieving myself, I am thinking what a shot in the dark this is and it's likely a total waste of time. I should have called Alexandra to meet me here, thinking to myself of course, that's probably a longer shot in the dark. In fact, I don't really know if the "jump right in" girl is a student, much less a student at Loveland or even a student that likes to go to the Study Place on a Friday afternoon, one week before Thanksgiving. Maybe she is dating one of the players, who knows, probably had a better chance of Alexandra meeting me here. When I come out of the bathroom, I look around and all the tables are taken. Damn, I am thinking, should have left something behind to keep the squatters away. I had a table, gone now. I decide to leave, go see what the boys are up to and blow off this waste of time. As I am leaving, about to push the door open, I hear my name, "Brandon," at least I think I hear my name. "Hey Brandon" then louder, "hey, numb nuts" I turn around clearly identifying myself to everyone in the room as the one with numb nuts. There she is, the Rip girl, the Loveland Tiger, sitting at my old table, now her table, our table. Everyone in the coffee shop is looking at me, "Branded" I am thinking, is not the nickname they will remember.

Almost before I sit down, "How could you be so, careless?" she says with an aggressive whip-like voice, pulling herself out of her own chair toward me? "How could you be so stupid; the Computer Assemblers now know you exist. You went into it and came back out before fulfilling the mission. The Assemblers now know you exist; they are already on it."

Of course, her low range ranting and raving seems totally non-sensible to me as I look at her dumbfounded, mouth open. She continues her rant but a little calmer. "Well at least the second time with Maude you connected the memory, performed the task, fulfilled the mission. They probably don't know who you are yet but almost certainly tracking has begun. Don't you know the Assemblers are relentless, the Assemblers never stop   searching, they are computers, and your footprint has been recorded; they know you exist," she finishes.

Of course, like any sixteen-year-old, my first thought, as my mouth begins to close, this girl is cute, possibly really cute, maybe even hot. Then I try to shake my brain loose, focus, even listen. What did she say. Did she really just say all that to me? Why is this cute maybe even extremely cute girl lecturing at me? Yes, at me. Then I get it together, as my dad would say, "get your hormones under control, Junior." I remember her leap into the rip, the cut. We have something in common, something very different, very strange in common.

So, the first thing out of my mouth: "What the heck is an Assembler?" I ask, almost yelling.

She settles back to her chair. Processing my question, she realizes I am being honest; I really don't know, I am new to her world. She probably remembers when she was like me and new to the Rip world. Her reply is more subdued, more like talking, trying to settle me down.

"From what I have been able to find out they are computers, nothing else just computers, and they exist for no other purpose than to track down people like you and me. No clue where they might be located, but the tracking starts when you attempt to close the memory lost in time. when we connect the memory that should have occurred but for the virus. Please be more careful next time," she says again. "As far as I know, there are not that many of us around, not that many left."

"What's the big deal?" I say when she looks at me shaking her head.

"If they find you, you are gone, you will disappear,"

"You mean like kidnapped or dead?" I say.

"Not kidnapped, not dead, gone, gone forever like you never existed," she now says, whispering, "not even Zuzu's pedals to leave behind in someone's pocket."

I recoil, lean back in my chair, somewhat on overload--too much going on and it's all strange. I take a deep breath, trying to relax.

"Can we step back a bit and start over? Hi, my, name is Brandon Fair, I am sixteen and go to Sycamore High School and you are?" As I reach my hand out to introduce myself, she says, "I know who you are, Brandon, and put your hand down. Sorry about the numb nut's thing, that was rude. My name is Julia Child, also sixteen, and as you know I go to Loveland High School."

For a minute I just stare at her, this time not because she is cute (which she is), But because I do not know what to say next.

Finally, I blurt out everything I can think of in shot gun style, everything that has happened to me since the weirdness began. Everything about the Rips, the pole, the accident, Maude, seeing her, seeing her jump into a Rip, kissing Johnny, Johnny as a policeman and more. I go on for many minutes and then just shut up. Shut up and shut down, tired, I could use something to drink I think to myself.

"Finished, would you like something to drink or eat?" she says, staring at me.

"You kissed Johnny?" she blurts out. We both stop, look at each other and then burst into laughter; we can't stop. Laughing helps, laughing feels good. The laughter relaxes both of us.

After what seems like forever, we gain control of ourselves and settle in and Julia asks, "Why do you call them Rips?" We are now thirty minutes into conversation with donuts and coffee busy talk to get acquainted, same shop, same Friday afternoon.

"That's what they look like," I reply, "at least to me. What do you call them?" I ask.

"Nothing. I don't call them anything, I don't have a name for them, seems kind of goofy if you ask me."

I look at her and say, "Well, you have clearly been doing this goofy thing longer than me. When I saw you, you leaped into, 'it' emphasis on 'it,' you leaped into the Rip with great confidence, no hesitation and clearly knew what you were doing, what you were getting into. Do you also become a dead person like I did, do you feel you are inside the person but still know who you are?" I finish and ask.

"I think so," she says. "The Rip, as you call it, is like a virtual cut on your hand or leg. The Rip is like an open wound in time. From what I have come to know, the rip or tear represents that unfulfilled desire or duty of the person who has the virus. A rip forms or develops because an event that was supposed to occur may now never occur. It leaves a hole in time and as far as I know loaders and linkers like you and me connect the memory of the actual event that should have occurred. We become the person to enable the connection to the lost memory. Does that make sense?" she asks, looking right at me.

Oh yeah perfect sense--we are both wacko, nut jobs, I am thinking to myself now. I am back to square one, not confused really but dazed and on overload. Assemblers, Linkers, Loaders, viruses. I need a little more guidance, I am thinking, a little more input, more data, "Yeah....," I say in a drawn-out elevated manner as if she has a duty to go a little further and tell me a little more.

"All right I get it," she says. "The virus is attracted to everyday life. It attacks emotional thoughts or desires, targeting everyday life events of everyday people. In that way the virus is diabolical. The world changes slowly, methodically without rhyme or reason it ruins lives one at a time, day after day. No one ever notices, no one knows except of course, us, Linkers and Loaders. We see the Rips and we know what they represent. If we don't succeed in our mission, if we don't connect or fulfill the person's memory to the lost moment, the Rip will close. The virus is successful, and time is changed forever. In your case Maude dies at the crash, Johnny never wakes up, he never takes the test, Johnny never becomes a policeman."

Julia leans back now. "That's about it most of what I know in a nutshell," she concludes, as if everything she has said is normal, expected, and we can now go on with our everyday lives, all just fine and dandy. Then she says in trailing, kind of an afterthought, "I think this whole mess, the whole shebang; the creation of the virus, Assemblers, Linkers, Loaders; you, I and even Ming's all stems from some Indian Company screwing around with biogenetic research right here in Loveland over a decade ago. They did top secret research for the Federal Government." My mouth now hangs open again, Venus fly trap like.

"Ming's," I say. "Who or what is a Ming's?"

Chapter Three

"A loader is responsible for loading executable files into memory. It calculates the size of a program (instructions and data) and creates memory space for it and initializes various registers to begin execution."

Before Julia and I leave the coffee shop, we come up with a game plan; communicate by texting, no phone calls, meet at various days and times. We agree no parents as she has none; she is living with her uncle. No friends either, unless of course they are one of us, no more jumping until I meet Ming's, yes, Ming's.

Ming's, it appears, may be one of us. Ming's was first, she believes, before Julia. He is how Julia got up to speed. Ming's was the key. Julia indicates she does not know if he will meet with me; he is reclusive, cautious, but very smart, very knowledgeable as he has history and knows a lot about the virus. She does not know his real name, and she is not certain why he knows a lot. She believes it stems from his father's work at a small University in Eastern Europe. Ming's is likely Asian and older than us, Julia thinks, but he doesn't look it. He is small, no, she corrects "not small, but slight, maybe sickly" but she's not sure. Julia does not know where he lives, if he goes to school. She calls him Ming's because that's where they first met, at Ming's Chinese Street Food Diner in Loveland and that's what he asked to be called.

"At least we know where you and I should meet next," I say out loud.

Of course, it wasn't lost on me that Julia tagged Girta at the coffee shop. I just didn't want to shout out, "that's Girta, that's probably Binky," That's me, that's my mom. I bit my tongue until I could think about it and get a plan together, not the least of which would be figuring out what role Binky might have played, what she might have been up to? In addition, how do I know if Julia is on the good side, my side, the right side? I don't know anything about her.

So, I decide to start my search in the obvious place, our attic, where Ron, my dad, has stored all of what is left of Binky. I found her sealed box, duct taped, and properly identified and stacked in the attic just where dad said it would be. As I mentioned he is very organized. I opened it up and started searching through it for some reason very carefully, methodically, like it is all made of glass but there is no glass, nothing really but books, pictures, office stuff and useless knick-knacks. My dad had warned me, "There won't be much all personal stuff. I removed that before storage then Girta came and did a complete sweep of Binky's materials when she died. They had a professional crew come to the house. TC, the owner kept apologizing over and over for the inconvenience, the intrusion. I believe he genuinely liked Binky, and he missed her very much. He told me they were required under the Federal Contract to search for and recover any work-related materials. Binky's work was a part of a highly sensitive program for the National Institute of Health, a specialized arm of the NIH," Ron said.

Whatever, I am thinking as I keep probing through the neat, organized stacks inside the box. There are a couple of novels stuffed away. I page through a couple and put back down then I pick up, *For Whom the Bell Tolls*, there is a note to me written on the cover. Right there on the front cover are you kidding me, "Keep Reading, Brandon, Love Binky, your mother." Wow, something from her ten years ago for me, her handwriting, her thoughts, just for me. I don't realize until a tear hits the page that I am crying.

"Crap," I say out loud while quickly wiping the tear off the page and closing the book. I sit there for a moment to get myself together, then quickly glance at the back page of the book again-her handwriting and a message for me, "Keep Reading…" I really don't remember her reading much to me or encouraging me to read but don't remember much at all about her. I was like five or six at the time. She probably read one of her science journals to me. I decide that's enough for today. At sixteen I am way too old to cry over this kind of stuff. I put everything back exactly the way it was with the tape seal back in place and the box back in its designated spot. Dad would be proud. I put the Hemingway book in my back pocket and left the attic.

Days later I am sitting on the floor at the gym when it hits me practice has just ended, and I am soaked; we worked out hard. Alexandria, my hopeful significant other, has already left her volleyball practice in the adjacent gym and now over, just a quick wave from the back as she exited. Things with her aren't going quite as planned. Oh well, I am thinking my head is elsewhere.

Binky never really read to me, I think and say over and over but I can't get it out of my head. My only recollection: she got home late, up early, left for work, always gone, always working. The note is at the end of the book, not the beginning." Keep Reading, Brandon, Love Binky," I repeat that over and over. The note on the cover of the book. Maybe it's not encouragement, I think to myself, maybe she is not trying to encourage me. She is not trying to encourage me to read more maybe she is trying to tell me something, maybe she is trying to get me to listen. It's a message, I think it's a message, she wants me to keep reading the book, this book-maybe even the others, there is something about the book. Ten years later stored away, in a sealed box, under a pound of nothing, hidden by five hundred plus pages a message from my mom right there in front of my nose.

Back in the safety of my room, I am farsighted so grab my glasses. I have looked through the book a couple of times, even read a spot or two of various chapters, nothing. Then I noticed something as I was fanning the pages - a smug or smear, what is that? I work my way back in the book to the page. I knew it, I just knew it, pure Binky, there it is on page 57. My tear drop gave it away. When I wiped my own tear away, I wiped away ten years of cover. Behind the book print, behind the print is another set of words--a message, she left me a message. This is too James Bond. I close the book, open it back up again to page 57, close it again. I look around suspiciously, although I am alone in my room back home, now what?

I have a small paint brush from a cabinet downstairs and a glass of water. I open the book and turn to page 57 and gently start…careful not to use too much water. Don't ask me why, I have never done this before, maybe I saw it done in a movie or show. I even find myself stroking upward from bottom to top, from right to left—go figure. Something about lemons and a hair dryer comes to mind, not sure why but this is working. The print behind the print is beginning to show. I blow on it just to dry it but also thinking I should take my time. Too much water or going too fast might cause damage that I don't understand. At first glance I think the writing might be from her work.

What I can see is a few half sentences, even bullet points, they are short and incomplete. I only have about a small mid-section of page 57 exposed. The older smudge from my tear is lower right to the page. I'm trying to avoid the smudge from my tears for now. Page 57 is on the left side of the book, but I can only see half a sentence. I stretch the binding, push the book open and move to page 58, hoping to complete the sentence or thought and bingo, there it is, the first complete sentence comes together.

Kind of gobble gook looks more like a four -year-old banging on the keyboard. Panic hits.

"Crap," I say out loud. I hope Binky didn't go to all this trouble just to save some goofy memory of me playing with her computer.

However, as I look closer, I can see what looks like a bunch of words, one word after another, running together, real words with no spacing. Frantically, now looking for a pen to try and write the words out, no pens, no pencils anywhere, can't find a single one anywhere in my room. Then I remembered my dad's an accountant. He has coffee cups full of pens, pencils, markers, and highlighters like the back-to-school section at Wal-Mart even he won't miss one, so I ran to his office to get pen and paper.

I write down the sentence as it appears in the book: Anassemblertranslatesassemblylanguageprogramsintom achinecode,theoutputofanassembleriscalledanobjectfile whichcontainsacombinationofinstructionsaswellasthedat arequiredtoplacetheseinstructionsinmemory Then I write the sentence properly spaced (I think):

"An assembler translates assembly language programs into machine code the output of an assembler is called an object file which contains a combination of machine instructions as well as the data required to place these instructions in memory."

For Whom the Bell Tolls is a famous Earnest Hemingway novel. I really don't know if the actual novel has any significance. I think deep down it might. I also don't know much about how Binky died, but I know deep down I need to find out. A bell tolling is to mark the death of someone important, like Binky. So, I must come up with a game plan to dissect the book. I don't want the bell tolling on Binky's message to me and her hidden notes. How do I uncover what is hidden without damaging or threatening the content? I think I know where to start, at the end because that is where her blinking red light of a message was, so I decide to work backwards. Earnest Hemingway would be proud. he loved intrigue and adventure. My plan is to just touch each page in various parts with my brush, quick blots really to see if anything shows. If it does, I will dig in. For the first hour or so it is slow going, nothing I find nothing for 15-20 pages working in reverse and this is a long book. There are more than 500 pages. I'm alone in the house, working in my room, my dad and stepmom at work. I haven't mentioned much about my stepmom, Agnes. She is a good lady, great for my dad and good for me as she loves us both. She works at a local dress shop, "just to stay busy," she is fond of saying.

My thought was to tap and paint my way through the entire work before starting to take or interpret the notes. At the current rate, which is painstakingly slow, done by my next birthday, I think to myself more than little sarcastically. Everything is working smoothly, just slowly, not much progress or very little progress to show for the time and work expended. Clearly a good time for a break since I have basketball practice at five and next get together with Julia is tomorrow. Hopefully getting together with Ming's as well as she is trying to get a hold of him to confirm--but who knows? Among other things she has said he is reclusive.

The next morning Julia's text arrives.

"We are a go for meeting Ming's today around noon." Ming's in Loveland, Ming's the Chinese Street Food Diner hoping that Ming's, the person will be there. The restaurant is at the end of a short grungy strip center next to an Asian grocery, nail salon, and couple of empty spaces for lease. As I walk into the restaurant, I can see that it is somewhat crowded for noon on a Saturday. Mostly Asians from what I can tell. I didn't know Asian was popular in Loveland but again, I don't get out much. Julia is sitting at a booth along the window facing the door, no one next to her. I have not seen her since our last meeting just before Thanksgiving. There is someone sitting directly across from her. Both are pushed to the window side of the booth. I can't see who, but clearly male, dark short hair, bald spot on the back left side of the head shoulders barely clearing the back of the booth seat.

"Hi Julia," I say as I turn to face the table and slide in next to her. " You must be Ming's," I say, and this time do not offer my hand. He is wearing a light blue disposable face mask with thick round glasses. I think he smiles as he says without hesitation, "You're Brandon Fair, Binky Fair's son." It's not a question, he knows. I don't really catch this right away, but how does he know I am Binky's son? I am still taken back by his appearance. He is blotted or better said his skin is blotted. I can't tell how much, but it shows on the left side of his face and on the back of his head.

Not freaky by any means, but caught me off guard, along with the mask and glasses. He is small as Julia mentioned, larger than a child but much smaller than most of my friends and even Julia. All told at first glance his appearance is a little disconcerting. There is nothing in front of them; no drinks, no food; I can't tell how long they've been sitting here, but the waitress comes over as soon as I settle in, as Ming's finished addressing me, and hands us menus. She wants to know what we want to drink and order. Julia and Ming's indicate just water.

"Well, I am a growing sixteen-year- old," I say out loud. "Sorry guys but I'm hungry and need food." I don't know anything about Asian food, so I order a cheeseburger and sweet tea, "Please." Diane, the waitress writes this down and she is off. Julia waits until she is some distance away and nods at Ming's. it seems they have decided how to proceed once I arrived.

Ming's begins, no prompting from me. "My late father was an early pioneer of isolating messenger RNA and attempting to manipulate mRNA to influence viral consistency. RNA regulates how genes are expressed. He worked with a team of scientists at a University in Hungary. The team was mostly biochemists, and their work was considered experimental, mRNA research considered volatile, back then even somewhat uncontrollable, especially when you are attempting to alter gene sequence of existing virus or bacteria. The scientists working with it back then did not have the knowledge or technology they do today. Your mother, Brandon, Binky Fair, was collaborating with them here in Cincinnati through an NIH award to the Girta Technologies Company. Girta's work was funded through an agency of the Federal Government, a part of the National Institute of Health. Julia's mom also worked at Girta, but in what capacity I do not know," he says looking right at her. "I ended up here or my dad and I ended up here when Girta and Chemie Research merged, and at that point the technology center for this project became the Girta team. I worked with my dad for a time at the Loveland facility but left early to college and graduated from University of Dayton when I was seventeen."

"With honors I believe," Julia adds.

Ming's gives a quick look to her then continues. "Most of the time we lived in Dayton, my dad and sometimes I worked for another government contracting firm, somewhat like Girta. This firm had a minority owned contract with Wright Patterson Air Force Base to explore viral disease epidemiology. The focus was to study the distribution of viral diseases in populations." He finishes his summary and now looks at me.

Okay, I am thinking, I know some of what Ming's is referring to from what Ron has told me. I don't know anything about messenger RNA, sequencing virus or bacteria. I do now know Ming's has a "late" father, Binky died young, and Julia lives with her uncle-- parents I assume no longer with us. The Girta company appears to be the common link for all of us. I log these thoughts away for later but for now, I decide to go right to the guts of the matter.

"Well thanks, that background helps," I say to Ming's, "and it all sounds good, but can we get more to the point," I say. "What is a rip, why do I feel compelled to jump into one and why do I become the dead person?"

"Fair enough," he says. "Julia told me you call them rips or tears. If we are talking about the same thing, I believe your mother used to call them folds. At least that is the term I heard my father use, although he believed these things to be a figment of Binky's imagination. A rip or fold as I understand it," Ming's says, "results from the person whose memory was altered. The memory loss might now be permanent. It is possible the rip, as you call it, or fold as Binky called it, may represent a wrinkle in time, something that was supposed to happen but didn't. Maybe the Gods of Time know something is off kilter and assume there must be a fix available," he speaks. "There is, of course, a fix available; you, Julia and those or others that may be like you," Ming's continues, "think of a rip or fold as Mother Nature's way of expressing one last chance before the window closes. That, I assume is why you become the person. Why you are attracted to the rip is another matter, but clearly something in your and Julia's genetic makeup makes this available to you. Maybe we can just refer to them as Ripfolds, combining both your and Binky's thoughts to keep things straight?" Ming's says.

"Works for me," I respond, "Ripfolds it is."

"Remember," Ming's concludes, "I cannot see and therefore cannot enter one, therefore it is unlikely that I am infected with the virus."

He continues, "According to my father's notes and our work together, the material objective of the University in Hungary and the Girta team was to develop a treatment, a vaccine, in the form of a pill or injection.

"The target was to help someone to forget, for the short term at least, a horrible event or a tragic memory for the purpose of treating--curing these issues. Things like; post-traumatic stress disorder, a result of war, mass shooting or death of a loved one. The Girta team was part of this research. Girta also believed messenger RNA showed great promise for broader medical application. Girta was actively experimenting outside of the contracted scope of work. Binky, your mother called the research in this area "Object Event Viral Research," Ming's concludes, checking on my reaction. I make a mental note to look for this in the book, in Binky's notes hidden behind *For Whom the Bell Tolls*.

Ming's looks at me, hesitates to see if I am taking any of this in or maybe going over my head. He seems satisfied and continues. "Object Event Viral Research is a little like the Gain of Function research popular today. Gain of Function in today's research generally refers to a process in which scientists implant or modify viruses with new properties to alter the genetic messaging, presumably to focus the virus on a new outcome or a specific outcome, a desired outcome. Hopefully something positive happens or occurs, but nonetheless an outcome foreign to the natural occurring virus. Object Event Viral Research with messenger RNA was the early predecessor to the Gain of Function research. It is thought that a mutated virus was created either intentionally or at random as a direct result of Gita's early work with mRNA.

However, this man-made virus had a mind of its own, the virus being drawn to or driven by the emotion of the host to attack memory. The host in this case being the test animal that was injected, typically primates. It was attracted by the emotion of the carrier, the monkey, a desire in the primate to do something, no matter how simple. An emotion so strong in the host the virus is attracted to it. The virus then latches onto the object or action and in my understanding, this resulted in changing the intended action or event, resulting in a broken memory. Now a missed action or moment changing the course of history for that isolated event, for that person, for that family. Assuming, of course, treatment could someday be applied and used by humans instead of monkeys."

Ms. Spragen, my ninth-grade teacher, her favorite saying was, "for every action there is an equal and opposite reaction," although, it seems, most often she was referring to something stupid one of us kids did. Boy, did she get that right in this case. Ms. Spragen's rule seems spot on. I don't grasp all the technical jargon, but I understand enough.

"Okay," I say looking at Ming's and back and forth to Julia, "but we are people, Julia and I are people, just teenagers, not computers, not viruses, not messenger RNA. Why us and how on earth does this happen?"

"I don't know the answer to those questions," Ming's says. "My father was aware of some of the Girta research because of the merger of the companies. He knew, for example, that Girta abandoned its quest to discover new medical applications when they discovered it was causing unanticipated problems, uncontrollable problems."

"The rogue virus?" Julia asks.

"Yes, but there could be other problems we are not aware of," Ming's says. "Ultimately, Girta attempted to construct a computer using early artificial intelligence capabilities. We believe the Assemblers and Connectors, Brandon, that you have heard about. Binky and her team were trying desperately to find a solution, a solution to the unanticipated problems that emanated from their viral research, hopefully, to mitigate the issues and the consequences. However, at some point, the effort to mitigate the issues was abandoned as being too risky to uncontrollable," Ming's says. "Binky may have continued the research on her own in hopes of a proper solution or positive, controllable outcome. After all it was her service, her life's work. As to you and Julia, I think you were both somehow exposed or injected with something, a part of the research either intentionally or by inadvertent exposure. What has triggered these changes now in your life cycles I am not sure," he continues, "possibly puberty since this trait appears common in both of you."

As we settle in, I noticed a few things about Ming's. He is acutely aware of his surroundings. His eyes indicate maturity certainly, older than Julia and me, clearly more experienced, more educated than both of us. He is also, I think to myself, stronger physically than he appears, wiry and quick. I would guess, not sickly, his color, skin blotting is misleading. The skin blotting is distracting but not physical. He is clearly stronger than he appears and intelligent, intensely so. Moreover, he knows it and exudes confidence that is reassuring. He has also grown more comfortable with us and is no longer sporting the surgical mask finally, and maybe most importantly for me, I like him.

Based on what Ming's has now told us, it appears Julia and I might have different functions, different reasons to exist. Julia does not connect the action to the memory. She is more like data. She plants the memory or better said, the data associated with the memory that was lost or destroyed by the virus. This, again according to Ming's, sets the stage to allow Loaders like me to connect the memory to the final action. I briefly remember a sense I had when Maude and I backed out of the crash as if something clicked-for her, for Maude. Julia had been there before me. Julia and I are made for each other, literally. Ming's refers to her as a Linker, linking the lost data, according to Ming's. As a Linker she is probably safe from the Assemblers as she came later. They may not know she exists. They aren't programmed to find her, as her function was created in the labs at Girta to help solve the problem caused by the rouge virus. Whatever I am or whatever I am infected with already existed and therefore is already a part of the equation. He believes the Assemblers were the original link, remembering again the very first notes I uncovered in the book, on page 57, *For Whom the Bell Tolls* .... An Assembler translates assembly language programs into machine code the output of an assembler is called an object file which contains a combination of machine instructions as well as the data required to place these instructions in memory."

Ming's believes computer-generated Assemblers/Combiners became the trigger mechanism for releasing the virus used to change host memory instruction. Ming's also believes Loaders/Linkers' actions were likely invented or created at Girta, invented to replace the misguided Assembler mechanisms. As noted by Ming's, the idea to create an action to combat the effect of the virus was ultimately aborted, it becoming unclear to the people in charge, whether Assemblers, Loaders, and Linkers might make the problem worse maybe even cause the virus to spread unpredictably, creating and causing new issues, dangerous issues.

He believes but does not know that the Assemblers may be the ones responsible for closing the Ripfolds, their primary reason to exist. Their central programming, he believes, is to find and close all folds, to shut down the virus and its effect forever including anything associated with that function, like Julia and me. Remember Ms. Spragen's rule; every action causes an equal and opposite reaction. I made a mental note to learn more about Assemblers and Combiners-- it seems they represent a danger to me, maybe not to Julia probably not for Ming's.

I realize coming out of the meeting with Julia and Ming's I have a lot of to learn, a lot of work to do, more importantly I need to finish translating Binky's notes. The book and translation are taking me forever to finish, to unfold, thinking I would almost prefer to read the novel as I laugh to myself. I still have not attempted to translate many of the words, no spacing can really muck things up; however, with the background provided by Ming's and Julia's presence, I now have a better sense of what I am looking for. Being around Julia is a plus. It makes all this work easier. Many of Binky's notes use technical language that is unfamiliar to me and makes no sense, so every now and then I must retrace my work, take a few lines and write them out. Writing some of the phrases out helps me believe in what I am doing, helps me translate to something real. In this way I have begun to expose bits and pieces of her past work, now more and more like her life's service. Her life without me; I was just a kid.

Good thing I still have basketball, which I need to head out to soon. The season is going well for the team and myself as we have yet to lose a game. My coach tells me I am getting solid attention from numerous college scouts even as a sophomore. Glad to hear it and even happier that he deflects this for me. I've got enough to think about. "Bet I am the only sophomore prospect in the state that can jump through time, wait until Nike hears about that," I think and say out loud. This thought makes me laugh and stop for a second then put down my blot brush, thinking about my mother Binky. She died before I could really read, write, or even play basketball. Now I'm wondering, did she really think about me? Did she really hide all this for me to find, or is this just a wild shot in the dark for us? Hard imagining her working alone, in a dark room clandestinely duplicating and weaving her work into the confines of a bookshelf novel, thinking all along, "one day Brandon will find this information and he will…. and…he will… "he will what? What the hell was she thinking, what am I supposed to do with this information once it's uncovered? Of course, I'm secretly hoping this becomes self-explanatory, maybe get lucky and find the answers in the table of contents. "Brandon, for detailed instructions on the next step in your life, go to Chapter Three, paragraph sixteen or @brandongohereformoreonfolds," as unlikely as this may be.

However, one thought does come to mind, she knows or thinks I will be affected, or infected by her work. I want to believe this, want to believe the book is directed to me, why she went to all the trouble to do what she did. The more I think about this idea, the more comfortable I become. She must have believed that sooner or later I would have questions, things would happen, strange things would happen to me. I would come to know or realize I am different in this way. She left me guidance, reassurance. Maybe I also understand now I need some help guidance and reassurance from others and think I know just where to turn.

Neither Julia nor Ming's know about the notes that are a part of *For Whom the Bell Tolls*. It is time to share, they can help. Also thinking as I get up and throw the gym bag over my shoulder, it's also time to dig into Girta. Girta is where it all started. As I shut the front door behind me and head toward the street, off to practice, the same path I take almost every day, maybe a hundred times before, "For Whom the Bell Tolls, it tolls for the dead," I say out loud to myself, hope I don't hear any bells anytime soon, I am thinking.

Chapter Four

"An Assembler translates language programs into machine code. The output of an Assembler is called an Object file which contains a combination of machine instructions as well as the data required to place these instructions in memory."

Julia and I are sitting at the diner together waiting for Ming's. I plan to tell both about Binky's notes. I brought them with me, in my backpack. It's nice sitting next to her. I have grown to think of her as "Jules." Julia seems too formal to me. She feels electric, like one of the Ripfolds. I can feel and sense her energy. She has a way of making people feel good just by walking into the room. Always in motion, she likes to be active. She is short, tiny really, thick brunette hair, usually worn up on the top of her head, stream or two hanging this side or that, no lipstick little if any makeup. No jewelry, a casual shirt and jeans kind of girl, innocent, warming smile with big brown bug eyes. We have not spent much time together, so I don't know much about her. I'm hoping to learn more shoulder to shoulder now as we sit waiting for Ming's. I'm trying to keep the conversation going, so I ask her about the Ripfold journeys.

"It's like jumping out of an airplane," she replies, "But with skydiving you kind of know where you are headed." Julia talks with her hands, and as she says this her hand swings around, mimicking the leap and lands on mine. We both look down and then look up at the same time. I am not complaining nor planning on moving my hand. She smiles, laughs, and quickly lifts her hand and without missing a beat continues, "each time has been different for me, unique. My visits don't seem to last long, although I'm not sure time is relevant in the fold," she says. I ask while turning to look at her and still enjoying the shoulder to shoulder, "Do you become the person?"

"Yes, I think so," she says, "but saying it out loud makes it seem like such fantasy. Remember when Maude was stuck in reverse, that was me I was there," she adds. "At that point she knew," Julie says, "she knew what had to be done," we both now say out loud together.

As I mentioned, Julia and I are sitting next to each other in the booth leaving the seat across from us to Ming's when he arrives." Coming out of a fold is also kind of wild for me, it seems different every time," she says, just as Ming's walks in the front door. I hesitate a bit to respond to her as Ming's approaches. I add just as he slides into the empty booth across from us, "for me it is like being blindfolded and thrown off a speeding train." Ming's looking somewhat amused." Sounds dangerous," he says. We replay some of our conversation for Ming's, focusing on our common experience with Maude. He thinks and replies, "from what I know, this makes logical sense. As I understand it, the main function of a Loader (he looks at me) is to load executable files to main memory. The main function of a Linker (he nods in Julia's direction) is to generate or link executable files from object code, the data. The rest might be up to Maude, with a little nudging from Brandon," Ming's says. "This process is how computer memory is initiated, it's pretty standard if you know program language and machine code."

I jump in and say to both, "but I don't feel like I am doing anything inside of Maude I am just Maude, doing what Maude wanted to do. I have no sense of doing anything, directing anything, certainly nothing like manipulating or uploading data, uses and files as you say, Ming's."

"Ditto for me," says Julia.

"Let's face it, there is no logical explanation for what you two do," Ming's indicates. "As I mentioned it's possible, maybe likely both of you have been infected, programmed, or genetically modified in some way. Infected, programmed or modified to perform the linking and loading functions. Truth is we don't know, may never know. It would be good to know more. Girta, the local technology company, seems to be the common link for the virus and each of your parents seems like the logical place for us to start our inquiry," I then interrupt and say out loud, "Actually it seems to be the common link for all three of us," alluding to Ming's father, the merger and early work at University of Hungary. I am also thinking it seems like an obvious time for me to show the team *For Whom the Bell Tolls* to discuss with the team Binky and her notes.

I grab my backpack, pull out the book, put it on the table in front of us open to page 57 and push it to the center of attention. Both Julia and Ming's looking very interested, so I start talking.

"After my first meeting with Julia, I was a little shell shocked," I say. "I decided to begin digging into my mom's past and there was only one place in our house that contained anything to do with Binky, our attic. I pulled out her storage box with sheer luck found this book, more importantly then stumbled onto what was hidden inside, hidden underneath the intended text." Julia can see this because the book is facing us. As I look up at her, I can see now her mouth is hanging open. After a moment I turn the book around to face Ming's so he can now see the typed words in, around, and presumably behind Hemingway's intended verse. "I know it looks like hieroglyphics, but the words are not spaced properly. I have no idea why she would do this, but once you space them it begins to make sense," I say and simultaneously reach back into my backpack and pull out what little has been translated. I then handed the document to Ming's. He is clearly fascinated. Julia is looking at me, mouth now closed. She smacks me hard in the arm, calls me a jerk for waiting so long to show her. I can't blame her. It feels good to finally share with them, and I'm not sure where to go from here.

Ming's, having set the paper down, is now lightly paging through the book. It is obvious by his reaction he is very intrigued. "It is hard to decipher without the spacing," he states, so I jump in.

"The first clue I had of what was hiding behind the print appeared on page 57, but I decided to start at the end of the book to translate.

I just recently found the beginning, the beginning of Binky's notes as you will see, I think her work starts on page 11. Sorry it took so long to show each of you. It's kind of personal, and I didn't really know what I was getting into. You should also know that Girta did a complete sweep of our house when Binky died. My dad said this was required protocol under the government contract authorizing the work. She must have known her work was highly sensitive, she must have also known that if anything happened to her, the work might be seized and censored. Anyway, it helps me to think so because of the clandestine nature of the book and its purpose, not to mention the way she disclosed the existence to me. As you can imagine I was focused on why, assuming the notes would lead me to an answer to why I see Ripfolds and how we can do what we do. Was she behind it all maybe even up there directing us now?" I finish and the three of us now just looking at each other and the book and wondering what to do next.

Ming's needs to leave. He starts to rise and shoves the book in my direction. I pushed it back toward him, asking for his help. I ask him to take over the burden of uncovering the message, to help. He is happy, it seems, to have it back I can tell, happy to assume my burden, his reward, and then he is quickly gone. I hope I made the right decision as I look at Julia she and I now alone again, still on the same side of the booth. Julia looks right at me says, "We should jump together, go into a Ripfold together, as one. We both feel compelled to act someone or something needs us."

"Why not," I say out loud. I am also thinking to myself this might be my service, my life service, after all I am half Sikh, we need to mend the wound before the Assemblers close it forever, something good might happen. Besides, what could possibly go wrong? Julia shakes me like I am off in never-never land and she is bringing me back to the present.

"Brandon, wake up, let's skedaddle, let's get out of here," she says, now laughing.

As we leave Ming's Chinese Street food diner, Ming's our fearless leader, Binky's book in hand now long gone. I'm beginning to believe he might be our tracker, our link in the real world, starting to believe we can rely on him. Then as Jules and I step to the curb we both see it. We both see a Ripfold, there it is, weirdly enough right in front of another corner street pole, right outside the diner. Julia sees it, I can tell, thinking to myself, a pole.

"Not again," I say out loud. Julia hears this, looks at me (she is clearly the more adventurous one) and loudly responds, "what the hell, right?" grabs my hand without waiting for a response while she reaches for the Ripfold with the other. One hand holding onto me, one hand now approaching the Ripfold.

"Hey," I yell back, "this is like a first date!"

"You wish," is all I hear and Bang, we are gone.

This feels good we are running along an city street, mid-morning, warm and humid. The running is not full speed but steady, our breathing is heavy but not exhausting, nothing like sprinting up and down a basketball court. Thinking to myself, I am inside a Ripfold, inside a person, another person and we are running. Looking around as we move forward it appears to me, we are in a race the number 18 pinned on our shirt, labeled YMCA, not sure yet where we are, no signs or landmarks jump out at me, nothing recognizable nearby. The race is something like a 10k because there are other runners, all with numbers on their jerseys, runners of all ages, shapes, and sizes, nothing too intense judging from those around me. So, I am thinking community awareness fundraising type race. Two college age girls in front of me, heavy set woman to the left, what appears to be a whole family with a young man pushing a giant wheeled baby cart to the right of me. I turn; we turn our heads to look behind us and there are very few runners. We are clearly near the back of the pack and many of the runners I am thinking already across the finish line. Sizing up my own arms, hands, and legs; white male regular build, probably in my forties not quite sure yet but we are clearly not running to win.

I am looking for something, something I am supposed to pick up, something should be waiting for me at the mile marker six. We register this thought when we passed mile marker five, which was important to me. Oh no, I am thinking, I completely forgot about Julia. We held hands, we jumped together into this Ripfold, we should be in here together there should be three of us doing this run. This guy is lugging around some serious baggage, I think to myself. However, I cannot hear or sense Julia's presence. Maybe she is already gone or inside another runner. This thought causes me to look quickly at the other runners near Julia, I think to myself you there?

Silence, just somewhat heavy breathing from Olaf and the run, maybe she jumped out left the Ripfold without me I am thinking probably home watching tube, so much for our first date.

We are now approaching the finish line, the last few miles of the race. It went by fast. There are many people lined up along the finish line and there is one older gentleman waving at us from the sidelines, frantically waving at us and running along with us behind the first row of spectators. He is yelling, waving, his arms appear to be yelling right at me, "where is the backpack Olaf, why don't you have the backpack, what is going on?" he screams. Olaf and I look over at him. Clearly we recognize who he is and acknowledge him by waving back, more of an associate then friend Olaf is thinking, but familiar and the gentleman is clearly confused, even mad.

"Olaf," he screams, hands now high in the air waving. The backpack must be important, but we are through the finish line now and walking toward the main podium. All the runners and their family members are gathering, most runners are now finished but a few stragglers are stumbling across finish line. We continue to move to the middle of the crowd. The older gentleman who called me by name and frantically waving and screaming is nowhere to be seen or found. Olaf and I have already recovered from the run and breathing normally, looking around and enjoying the day, enjoying getting out and being a part of something. Why don't I do this more often, he is thinking. I have not been in the crowd more than a few minutes when it happens, we all hear it, we all hear a loud explosion behind us and some distance away. As the crowd turns to look, we can see smoke rising into the late morning sky. The explosion appears to be few miles behind us, too far away to cause immediate panic or concern. Clearly everyone is focused on it, and the man standing at the podium is looking directly at it, pointing at it and now everyone is wondering what just happened back there? Many started to disperse, some quickly, sign of the times probably. Olaf, you forgot the backpack, he thinks to himself. As this thought strikes him, as he remembers what he was to do, a moment of regret hits, and Bang I am gone.

Now back in my world after the run with Olaf and my first Ripfold journey with Julia, well kind of this time landing in a small patch of grass outside Ming's Chinese Street Food back to where we started. Not a bad exit this time, just a little "rug" burn. I quickly stand up, brushed off and walking toward my house while texting Julia.

"What happened Jules, were you there with Olaf and me?"

She responds almost immediately, "yes, but not for long I was gone right after we passed the fifth mile, what happened with you," she asks.

"Hard to say really but it appears Olaf and I forgot to grab a backpack during the race and right after the finish, with the race then over there was a loud explosion about a mile back."

"Wow" is the text she sends back. "This is incredible. Let's try to get with Ming's tomorrow night?" Julia then follows her last text quickly with, "I like it."

"Like what?" I respond.

"The nickname, Jules," her response. Then few minutes later, "let's plan on meeting at the diner at 7:00, after your practice, I will text Ming's," her last text back to me is signed, "Jules."

It is next evening. I just finished practice, showered, and just hanging out in the gym now watching the JV team run up and down the court. My friends know something is up. Jimmy has it pegged, he knows or assumes a girl is involved. Not hard to figure out since I disappear a couple times a week. I'm not sure what to tell him so for now, I just play along with the ribbing. It's not lost on my parents either. Both Ron and Agnes asked a lot of questions. Here I go again, I am thinking now looking around. No one in sight, time for me to skinny out the back of the gym and walk to Ming's, the diner. Jimmy and the boys are probably still in the locker room. I also need to text my dad let him know I'll be home late and will grab my own dinner.

Ming's reaction and response when he hears about Jules and I both jumping at the same time when he hears about the race, the explosion and our journey into the same fold together is a surprise to both of us. He is not amused, he is clearly alarmed; he thinks it is incredibly dangerous, "Cavalier really, each of you should know better," he says, sounding very concerned. It is likely he thinks the Assemblers and Compilers may now know there is another, there is a Julia. The footprint of both of us in the host at the same time might have raised awareness of Julia's existence. No matter how brief the visit, we need to be more careful in the future, he emphasizes to both of us.

Ming's other observation and concern more troubling to him, he points out the action we pursued is diametrically different from previous journeys." The opposite really, you caused the host to forget not to remember," he says.

" The man, it appears, was supposed to pick up the backpack, which was the memory. It appears, however, the two of you were the catalyst for him to forget, to run past the backpack and forget the action. This represents a new behavior, possibly a new direction. Maybe not so surprising," he indicates. "The natural tendency of any virus is to survive. To do this, they often change or mutate. Mutation is a form of survival for a virus. We may be seeing a new virus, a hybrid or something completely different emerging. In fact, there may be another possibility." Ming's stops and looks at both of us, trying to drive home the seriousness of his next comments. "It is possible," he says, "the two of you are the virus—I'm not sure how else what occurred with Olaf could happen. If this is correct, however, and the two of you caused the memory change, who or what created the Ripfold?"

Jules, the ever adventurous one, jumps in and says, "This could get really interesting." I am more practical, less concerned, and note to all there is some upside pointing out to Jules and Ming's, reminding them really, "one way or the other we likely saved the lives of hundreds of innocent runners and family members." This causes all three of us to stop, hesitate and reflect. "This," I say out loud, "is worth a toast." All three of us lift our water glasses and clumsily clank them together, throwing water in all directions. We laugh in unison then decide that's enough for one day." "Let's get out of here," Jules says.

Chapter Five

"A program is a set of instructions that tells a computer what to do. It instructs the machine to solve a particular problem."

All roads lead to Rome or in my house straight to the attic. I am upstairs once again sifting through Binky's box. It's late afternoon and an hour or two before I need to be at the gym. Big game tonight, we play Princeton. The big dog, the big kahuna, number one in the city, number four in the State, the Vikings are big, athletic, and quick. Even their cheerleaders can dunk, I think, laughing to myself. Up in the attic again looking for some easy history or roadmap to Girta. But considering Binky's last message to me, I am being more observant in my search now, carefully sifting through her stuff. Nothing yet, nothing to catch my attention, just looking for basics really. After about half an hour, all I came up with is the owner's name, Mr. TC Singh, the old address, and brief company description.

Well, it seems all roads in my house lead to my attic and to Google. I found very little in Binky's box, so I am back in my room "googling" for TC Singh. There is quite a bit of information. He has lived a full and committed life, a life of service, a wife and many children, distinguished career, long list of accomplishments, honoraria, Boards, and service committees. Pulling from his own newspaper quote other than his wife and kids, his most important contribution he feels was establishing a conduit between the Sikh community in Punjabi to Cincinnati because of his efforts our area has one of the highest concentrations of Sikhs in the State. To do this, he helped establish a church or place of worship, the "gurdwara" or "Gurdwara Sahib," according to Sikh doctrine. People of all faiths or no faith are welcome. So, I am thinking the

Cincinnati Gurdwara is where I will start my search for Mr. Singh. There is a large Gurdwara in Hamilton, Ohio about fifteen minutes by car from where I am now. It is called the Guru Nanak Society of Greater Cincinnati; Guru Nanak was the founder of the Sikh faith.

Interestingly, enough, I was born in Hamilton. My only real memories were wiffle ball games with a surrounding army of kids and learning how to ride a two-wheel bike soon after Ron and Binky moved us to Evandale. Sikhs do not a have a specific day of worship. I read however, Sunday appears to be the typical day to come together, support, socialize, and pray. Sunday it is, now I just need a ride—not walking to Hamilton.

It's a few days after my last trip to the attic and the Princeton game. The Vikings proved that talent is important, maybe more important than team. We were right on their heels until the last five minutes of the game. At that point bigger, faster, deeper took over and Princeton cruised to easy win. We played well. I played very well, my best game this year, and in three weeks we get them again, this time at home. Being at home might be the difference. I'm already looking forward to February.

When I wake up the next morning, I do the same thing I always do, swing my feet around to the floor, stretch my arms over my head and run my fingers through my hair, wake everything up. I do the same today, this morning, basic routine. Not sure why, but I look down at my feet--not part of my normal routine but routine enough. Part of my right foot is not visible. I rub my eyes twice. right side of my foot, the last few toes and then some still not visible as if someone or something took a big bite. In a panic, I bend over and grab my right foot. It is still there. I can feel it. I just can't see it. I straighten up, sit in bed, make myself take a few deep breaths then look again at the area where my foot is supposed to be. It looks black, looks like night. I am no longer panicked, more fascinated. I am assuming this is not for real, maybe some kind of response from my last Ripfold journey. Not quite like the Star Trek thing where Scotty beams someone up, they arrive at the transporter with parts missing or in a heap of goo. I reach over, release the charger from my phone to take a picture, thinking this should be interesting, click the camera, then open up the photo, all good nothing missing, the photo shows everything as is, at least as far as my right foot is concerned. Maybe I am thinking to myself it's a blood flow thing. I need to stand up, get my blood flowing then my foot will be there? I stand up, jump up and down for a bit then look down. No change well, I am thinking to myself, it's there even if I can't see it is. I wonder briefly if it's a foot problem or eye problem, thinking I need to talk to Ming's and Jules about this. I also need to get to school.

The next day Ming's, Jules, and I are back at the diner. I have decided not to share with the team my missing foot parts or my research of Mr. TC Singh, not yet at least. I started up the conversation. "When we first met Ming's, you referred to Julia and me as the possible fix. In some respects, maybe even the basic reason the Ripfolds appeared. We were there to fix the lost memory, the Gods of Time you said were giving notice something wasn't quite right, needed to be fixed and sending out a message for a solution, a solution like Julia and me. At the same time, you referred to others like us," I say as I look back and forth between Jules and Ming's, "Are there other people like Jules and me?"

Jules is silent and now, looking directly at Ming's,

"Yes," Ming's says and then goes silent for a few awkward moments and before he adds, "well maybe. Truth be told, we don't know for sure but there was another, we called him Jeeves, neither Julia nor I have heard or seen from him in many months. Julia told you about the Assemblers, we think the Assemblers may have found him. Jeeves, you should know, was about your age, and Girta prodigy," Ming's adds. "There could also be others like him, we just don't know, but it stands to reason there would be others. At one point, Girta had over 100 people working in the same building."

"It is possible," Jules says, "he may have been trapped or stuck in a Ripfold. It also possible he might still be there," says Julia.

"Alive and living in the same Ripfold, is this possible?" I say to both Ming's and Jules.

"We don't know if any of this is true, we don't know what happened, no clue as to whether he was trapped in a Ripfold or not, no clue if he is dead or alive or possibly just missing. For all we know his parents moved and he went with them. We just don't know what happened to him, he disappeared," Ming's finishes. This revelation is like a slap in the face to me. I knew what we were doing was risky, but now I realize the Ripfolds might be dangerous, even deadly!

So, I say to both, "How do we find him, how do we begin the search for Jeeves?"

"You can solve this, Ming's," I say out loud or at least put Jules and I on the right track to finding him.

Ming's wants to get back to business." Guys, finding Jeeves would be great, but we have some work to do, all of which may help us solve the riddle involving his disappearance.

"How about sighting locations?" Ming's asks. Ming's has been tracking our sightings of Ripfolds. Our first task each visit is to identify for him where we have seen folds. Ming's wanting to map these and start tracking them.

"Tracking might be step one in finding Jeeves," he adds. He pulls out the hard copy map we have been using, and Jules and I go to work on what we have seen. Once we finish, I ask Ming's about Binky's notes.

"Yes, after working with the book and translating your mother's notes, I have additional insight as to her work and what was going on behind the scenes at Girta," he continues. "Do you recall the first notes you translated from the book? They focused on the Assemblers, do you remember that?" He looks at me, not expecting an answer and then continues. "The Assemblers are a function of computer programming. If you think of the virus and what is going on in terms of computer memory, you can understand better what is happening, you can understand the function of the Assembler. The Assemblers translate language programs into machine code. The output of an Assembler is called an object file. An Object file contains a combination of machine instructions including the data required to place these instructions into memory. Object files in and of themselves are incomplete. Real workable machine code requires absolute memory for function.

"Absolute memory addresses aren't available in Object files. Memory to be properly restored in a computer must combine all Object files needed for the function, but in our case, in the case of the virus, one of the Object files is missing. The Assemblers have control, holding, concealing, or storing an Object file. These must be recovered and then loaded or connected with the other Object files. This is how the Assemblers know you exist. Julia recovers the missing Object files then connects them with the other Object files by placing these in the proper placeholder slots. They are then linked and loaded by you, Brandon, with a program allowing the action to be performed and the memory is restored."

That seems logical to me. I am thinking.

"So back to my original questions, how did Girta and my mother jump the virus from computer modeling to real life, real people, and restoring real memory?" I ask Ming's and Jules.

"Well as I have alluded to before, some of what you guys do cannot be explained with XXs and OOs. However, remember the messenger RNA I mentioned before?" Ming's says. "mRNA in the ordinary course of life. It takes its instruction from your DNA, all of us have DNA. You were born with it; Julia and I were born with it. We all inherited it from our parents. The mRNA gets its instruction from your inherited DNA. The mRNA then brings these inherited instructions to the cell ribosomes. Each person's cell ribosomes then use these instructions to make proteins. Every cell in the human body can make proteins. Proteins do most of the cells' work, proteins make up your hair, muscles, bones, and they allow the body to move. Proteins then go out and cause things to happen in the human body, sometimes good things and sometimes bad things. The wrong protein or folded protein and you end up with Parkinson's or Alzheimer's.

"The target objective of Binky and Girta's work was to reprogram cell protein production by influencing the message being delivered by the mRNA, thereby creating designer proteins. The protein is no longer programmed to do the wrong thing, or it is reprogrammed to do something different. Binky thought teaming computer programming capabilities; the Linker, Loader, Assembler functions we've been discussing with reprogrammed mRNA could eventually lead to groundbreaking medical treatment with focus on customized treatment plans for individual patients. Ultimately the patient could take a pill or be injected with the manipulated or coded mRNA," Ming's concludes.

Wow, all that was in her notes?" I ask.

"Well yes to some degree; however, remember I was somewhat involved? I probably have insight others may not have," Ming's says. "Today much of what she was investigating is possible. The science, however, even today still has a long way to go. That being said, I did not find anything that would lead us to what has happened to you and Julia, at least not yet. I have not uncovered and translated all the text, still have some work to do," Ming's concludes.

I am thinking to myself I have some work to do as well. I don't know much about Assemblers, I know nothing about Compilers, a term Ming's just used in his description, maybe gleaned from my mother's notes. Outside of Ming's, the only source I can think of is Girta Technologies, Mr. TC Singh, Owner, and CEO, it seems all roads now lead to Girta, not just to my attic or Google.

It's Sunday the last week of January. Ron is driving me to the Guru Nanak of Cincinnati in Hamilton, Ohio. He seems happy about it as I think he is glad that a piece of Binky may be growing inside me. He wants to detour slightly to Joyce Park. Joyce Park has been around for decades. I played my first tee-ball game here, Ron says, reminiscing as we pull up to the baseball fields parking area. Binky and he were both there to cheer and watch me play. The old field looks much like it was many years ago, and hasn't changed much, just like the game of baseball. Baseball was his thing. Ron pitched in the Air Force; Ron doesn't understand basketball; he didn't grow up with it. After a minute or so he just shakes his head. Not much else to say, and we are back on the road again.

We find and turn into the Hamilton, Gurdwara Sikh place of worship. I ask dad if he would mind dropping me off and he seems fine with this. "Back in an hour or so," he says. As I walk around the Gurdwara I cannot help but think of my mom and wonder to myself if I might belong here, if this is my extended family. As I approach the temple or worship house, there are five or six men standing around talking. I am a bit nervous as I approach the group, saying out loud, "Excuse me I am looking for Mr. Singh?" Of course, all of them turn around at the same time. Should have seen that coming, "Sorry gentlemen, Mr. TC Singh," I clarify with a bit more confidence. One of the men comes over and kindly introduces himself. Javit Singh is his name. he asks me to follow him." I believe TC is inside," he says.

We walk in silence for a few minutes and are about to enter through one of the four main doors when Javit explains that it is custom before entering the prayer hall to cover our head with a cloth. He hands me a scarf and helps me place it securely on my head. As we enter the prayer hall, we stop to remove our shoes and wash our hands. The inside of the gurdwara is beautiful with a very ornate temple or altar in the middle of the hall. From what I can see, there are no idols, statutes, or pictures.

There is another smaller group of men off to the left side, and Javit leads me to them. "TC," he says as we approach the three men. "This young man is here to see you." Now walking up to him, I offer my hand, "Mr. Singh," I say realizing I did it again." Mr. TC Singh," I quickly clarify, "my name is Brandon Fair. My mother Binky used to work for you at Girta." TC looks up, sees me, and connects almost immediately. He is clearly taken aback, a look of shock maybe, even wonder on his face, but clearly he is elated to see me. He grabs my hand with both of his. He is not used to being surprised and not sure what to say, but he quickly recovers with no less warmth on his face than before. He is clearly very happy that I came to see him and said so numerous times. He wants to spend some time visiting, perhaps a whole evening, if possible. He says, however, prayer time is starting and there are no visible places to sit. He explains later there are no cushions and seats in a Gurdwara, so he takes me aside, gives me his contact information, and makes it clear he would like me and my father to come to his home for dinner. "That way we will have ample time to visit," he says." Call me soon, very soon, don't wait too long," he emphasizes.

It's been a couple of nights now since I had dinner at Mr. Singh's. My dad was unable to attend. He dropped me off, and one of TC's sons drove me home. I won't say the dinner was uneventful, but not quite what I expected. I was hoping there might be a few answers to my recent unique changes and challenges. Mr. Singh, however, has had some recent serious health issues, a stroke for one, which affected his stamina, memory, or ability to recall events beyond the most recent. He also emphasized that it has been some time since he was involved, as he sold the company many years ago.

However, there are two things I won't soon forget. First, he pointed out that Girta maintained a warehouse in an industrial area along Wooster Pike near downtown Cincinnati. He believes this may still be active because he still gets monthly invoices, which he promptly throws away, indicating that he would be very grateful if I could help clear this up. His wife promised to send to me the next warehouse mailer they receive. Mr. Singh's only recollection of the Wooster Pike location is that it was used for storing old files and outdated equipment, like computers. He thought at one point he probably owned the warehouse, believing now it was sold as part of the sale.

The biggest surprise of the evening came at the end as I was getting up to leave while I was waiting for Mr. Singh's son to grab his keys to drive me home. Looking around to fill the void, I started looking at the photos on the table behind the couch, some big names, some very recognizable faces. President Barrack Obama for one, but there was another picture more important to me, more recognizable to me. There was Ming's. A picture of Ming's in one of the framed photos sitting on the table. He is younger and next to him, I assume his father, with the Girta Corporate sign and building prominently displayed in the background. I would guess Ming's was probably my age at the time. The handwritten message in the lower right-hand corner read, "Thanks for Everything TC" signed by both Paul and Peter Huang. Peter "Ming's" Huang, the one and only. I took out my phone, snapped a picture of the Huang's, put the phone back in my pocket just as Mr. Singh's son returned from the kitchen, keys in hand ready to take me home.

Chapter Six

"The main function of the Linker is to gather and generate executable files from Object Files. Whereas the main function of the Loader is to take these executable files and load to main memory."

My name is Claude Turkett. I am old, old but look good, still look good and don't feel so bad. Occasionally I wake up with bad headaches, but that comes with the territory. I've got a few things going for me; I've got more than enough money, still drive, dress myself, still live alone. If you are laughing, you're likely young, age hasn't dragged you through the muck yet, but it will if you are lucky. I can still drive to my favorite restaurant, no chauffeur, order, eat, drink, and enjoy the commotion. I can't hear very well, so commotion rather than conversation is what I enjoy. Laughter is good. I can laugh with anyone. It feels good even if I don't really hear what is so funny.

Conversation is a challenge. Kind of sucks; I would love to just have one conversation where I heard it all, better if I understood it all but hell, I am over ninety years old. Life could be worse. I've got friends, got acquaintances and people to hang out with; most importantly, still got my freedom. I can decide when and where to go on my own, don't need to ask anyone. I don't need to check in at the front desk or sneak out to my car. Some things are hard. I don't understand things like I used to, but I'm not about everything. Some things you don't forget like ladies, women, girls. The good news is they are all young women to me. Still wonderful, smell nice, still grab your attention, a cute smile from a pretty woman still makes you feel good.

I am beginning to understand what has happened. The Ripfold has thrown me inside of him, the man is old but doing pretty-well.

He is thinking about his life, friends and health. There is one young lady, Claudes thinking starts up again, who has been around me for many years, friends only but she goes out of her way to find me no matter where she is; on her way home, on her way to a party or off on a date, she tries to find me. Of course, I am not that hard to chase down. There's only one restaurant or two close enough for me to wander into. When she shows up, she is usually in good spirits, happy, smiling, and friendly, she never fails to come over and hug me, hold me, laugh with me, and listen to me. An old man: me, the old man. She kisses and hugs me hello and goodbye. She is young, four of her would fit in my lifetime with years left over, but I like all of it.

I know now, however, my days here are numbered. Not because of death, although that's knocking too, but because my freedom is moving closer to family. My son has decided I can't live alone anymore, probably because I fell a couple of times; once in the garage, which hurt like a son of a bitch, once again in the kitchen. Inches from the marble corner tabletop, which would have knocked me silly, maybe back to God. Since my son and his family live in another town, that's where they want me and my freedom. Hard to argue with, especially when you are ninety, they want me closer to where they can watch over me, probably help me, keep me company, love me, spend time with me, hold me and my freedom, giving it back to me when convenient. I'll probably need to learn how to sneak out, sneak around maybe buy one of those fancy electric cars that don't make any noise when you back up.

I would like to do something for her before the Lord takes me home. Mona is her name. Believe it or not, it's not so easy for an old man to give a young girl a gift. People will think she snookered it. People will think she sucked me in, maybe pretended to like or even love me possibly even shared a body part or two. In this case, that could not be further from the truth. She is just a friend that shared time with me. You learn as you get older and realize nothing is more important than time and sharing it with others. Lots of people think love tops the charts, but they are wrong. It's not whether you are loved, it's whether you are needed. Being needed tops the charts. Being needed gives you purpose; without purpose you are not needed; nobody cares if you are at the restaurant, nobody cares about what you eat or that you dressed and drove yourself. More importantly, nobody wants to hear what you have to say, nobody asks your advice. Nobody wants to hear how you kicked ass when you were younger. You battled just like the younger guys do, no amount of wine, whiskey or woman can make up for that emptiness. Someone who needs you is important, take my word for it, it gives you purpose and hope, enough said.

Our minds aren't syncing but I can feel his thoughts. He is trying to figure out how to give his watch to the young lady. I don't think for any reason other than a gift. He thinks it can change her life. It's a Daytona. Paul Newman and I make it more popular every day we are thinking together. I don't think my son remembers, but Mr. Newman gave me the watch many years ago. We installed the artisan tiles in his Westchester farm homes. I ran a large artisan tile company in Monterey, Mexico for many years and got to know a lot of famous people, Paul and I got to know each other well. We went riding and shooting together, Paul being a good rider not much of shooter.

Now trying to give the watch to Mona without someone claiming, believing, or implying that she stole it, I'm back to snookered again. It's not easy when you're an old man and she is cute young lady. I have it in my hand now, then for whatever reason it comes to us, strikes us we know just what we're going to do with it.

Later that night we are lying in the dark--well I think it's dark. I should make sure my eyes are open, not sure if I am outside or inside. My last recollection taking care of Mona's new Rolex, my Rolex, hiding it at the bar, making final rounds to leave, telling everyone, "Glad you got to see me." Of course, at my age that could have been last week rather than today. I enjoy saying that every night. It pisses some of the older guys off, but it's my trademark, it's what I say, "glad you got to see me me, our minds repeat together.

There is a vague recollection in my mind that I was just leaving the Italian restaurant I like to visit, think I fell down the small loop of stairs to handicapped parking. Handicapped is where my car is parked, but it's hard to say. It feels nice just lying here, but I think I hit my head hard when I landed. It feels kind of like a warm shower, probably raining lightly, bleeding somewhere or I might have peed myself. Look like an idiot I'm sure, but oh well, I am ninety, I can get away with just about anything.

As I lay there, a bit of remorse hits. I'm worried that I still have not given Mona my Rolex. She needs it. She can use the lift, I think. Her life is just one party after another, she is easily distracted; of course, everyone is a distraction at her age. But she has some foundation, some footing. She is a talented hairstylist, at least I am told the only time she ever touches my head is to muss my hair, what little there is, but I believe it because many of the women I know go to her for fixing. Used to go, I should say, to her" parlor." The shop she worked for is now closed. In any event here I lay, and only the Lord knows if I am getting up. Now someone is leaning over asking us something. I should whisper something profound and freak them out. I can't really think of anything but "glad you got to see me," and "can you give Mona my Rolex watch?" I know it doesn't come out that way. Whatever I do say comes out garbled." Put it on the hanger," "at the bar I force out, "One of those hangers at the end," I think I say. It would be nice for her, give her a chance to make a change, and this might be just the thing. Not sure what it is worth today, but you can buy a house with a little bit of gold these days. It doesn't matter, it's more than she has now, lots more and it's what she needs to get her a new start and get away from the riffraff she is attracted to. With what energy I can muster I tell the face leaning over and looking at me hoping I don't forget.

"Hey, I don't care what she does with it, just the decision will be good for her maybe great for her." "Dad, it's me, Claude Jr.," I hear him say, "you are here in your bed, all of us are here," he says. Jr,' s hand is now on our shoulder. Claude Jr's hand is touching us I can feel it. It feels good, so I grab his arm with my right hand and squeeze hard. I want him to remember this moment. Something passes between us something important. I hope he got the message about Mona; the bar, the watch, and her future are all he was thinking. I hope Jr. gets the message he says before closing his eyes forever.

I jumped a Ripfold this morning as Jules has been on me lately for not committing myself to our calling, our service. In my mind I know this is important; it is important to restore the memory that the virus stole but I feel like there must be more. There must be a bigger picture, a better solution. We can't spend the rest of our lives jumping into one Ripfold after another. The weird part I think the old man just spit me out. Sent me off into his son. I think I am now inside Claude Jr. It feels very different our minds already syncing but with the old man didn't feel a thing. No communication formed between us. With Jr. this feels normal.

The two of us Claude Jr., and me staring down at his dad. There is no doubt I am no longer in him I am in his son. Wait until Jules hears about this. We can jump to others inside a Ripfold. Must have been when he grabbed our arm. He is gone now I feel his son thinking. When his life slipped away grabbing our arm threw me into Jr. Just as the Lord took him home he grabbed our arm, I am thinking. I know the memory we are to repair but he is no longer alive to do what the virus stole away from him, but I know what to do.

Claude Jr., and I now walking into an Italian restaurant on the far west side of Cincinnati. His dad is now deceased, and this was his dad's favorite restaurant. His father had an accident in the parking lot a few days ago and never got better. Jr. now has to deal with his estate; the old man had a lot of assets. As we enter the restaurant, Claude sees the owner, and we walk over to him now, reminding him of Claude Tuckett and that I am his son, Claude Jr. He instantly smiles, jumping to give me a long hug. He loved Claude, my father. Many of the people at this bar loved Claude. There is one person I am here to see, we say, but I don't know her, she has been described to me. Mona is her name. I was told she was here tonight, as the bartender called the hotel returning my earlier message. I'm not sure how long he indicated so I came right away. I was hoping to find her before I went back home. I don't plan on coming back anytime soon.

In any event, the owner leads me to the far side of the bar. He has known Mona for many years and is leading us to deep corner, narrow passage between the wall on one side and bar top on the other. There is a young girl there talking with a couple of older gentlemen. I recognize both Bob and Tim. Tim is clearly the older of the two, but I recognize them both. They were good friends of Claude's. They took care of him as needed when he lived just down the street. Bob was his attorney for a thing or two, and both attended his eighty-eighth birthday party. It's where the three of us met. They didn't recognize me at first. When I introduce myself, they both light up with large smiles to greet us. They are clearly moved. No one really knows what to say when someone's mom or dad has died but they are doing their best. I ask them how they are doing, great is all I hear. I also ask them if by chance they know Mona.

"She is right here," Tim says, "right next to me." As he turns to look at her, she is in an active conversation with one of the bartenders. Beautiful sunny smile, quick laugh, immediately we can see a little of what Claude loved. She is the last person standing at the very end of the bar toward the wall, so I squeeze past Tim and Bob and wait for her to turn. She just stopped talking to the bartender so I Introduce myself as Claude Turkett. Mona turns pale, almost white, "Claude Jr.," I say before she passes out.

Then almost in the flash of an eye the color is back. She is maybe 30, probably younger, likely mid to early 20s when she met my dad. Without hesitation I reached next to her and under the bar. This sudden move makes her a little nervous, and she backs away a bit. Tim and Bob are also wondering what we are doing. My right arm and hand feel around under the bar top and sure enough there it is. It feels like a sort of crook, not quite a hanger. Just where dad said it would be we are thinking. The restaurant owner may want to talk to his cleaning service. I pull my arm up from under the counter and in my hand is dad's Rolex watch. The Daytona, he used to call it, something he and Paul Newman, the famous actor had in common. We hold the watch up to our ear. "I hope Timex doesn't mind, but the watch is still ticking, well not really ticking. Rolexes are made too well to make noise as crude as a tick.

"Here it is," Jr. says aloud as he and I hold it up for all to see like the first gift of Christmas. Now I turn to show it to Tim and Bob and tell everyone within ear shot, "this is Claude's, my dad's Rolex watch. Believe it or not he left it hanging here the day of his accident, the day he passed." Everyone is stunned. "In all honesty, not even quite sure how I know of its existence. I think my dad was trying to tell me about it just as he died but when I woke up today and knew it was here. When I woke up today knew what I had to do," Claude Jr. says for all to hear. Together we now turn toward Mona, holding out the watch to give to her. She is looking at us as we do this.

"Here Mona, this is yours, my dad wanted you to have it." We try to hand it to Mona, but she is not prepared for the weight. Rolex watches are heavier than they appear; actually, gold is heavier than it appears. The watch drops directly to her napkin. Mona hasn't picked it up yet. She is just staring at it like it might start breathing. Well, she had better start breathing, we are thinking because she hasn't since the watch hit the bar top. Claude Jr. and I look at Tim and Bob and then, back to Mona.

"Well, that's the only reason I came here tonight. Good to see you guys again and finally meet you, Mona. I know why dad believed you were special. At this point the entire bar is watching the interchange. Before I leave," Jr and I announce loudly to all that can hear, to all sitting around the bar. "There is only one other thing," we announce. "One other thing we want to say to each and every one of you, 'glad you got to see me,' we scream loudly together." And for a moment, for just a flash, Claude Sr., is standing in front of everyone. The old man is there for all to see one last goodbye to all his friends. Then he is gone.

Now with a warm smile for everyone Jr,. and I begin to leave the bar. At the same time, Mona, now smiling, catches her breath. She moves her hand to cuddle the watch with her fingers, Wrapping the watch band, she sees an inscription engraved inside and begins to read aloud for Tim and Bob and the others to hear, "Glad I got to know you, Claude, "PLN," she says, "me too," she, Tim and Bob whisper together.

Then Bang I am gone.

Jules and I are walking to the diner to meet Ming's. My Ripfold visit with Claude and Mona is now a few days behind me. The fact that I jumped from one body to another inside the Ripfold still fresh in my mind. It's mid-February and light snow is on the ground. The roads and walks are clear, no wind, cold but nice outside. It feels good to enjoy a few minutes together. We are in no hurry, no practice tonight and her uncle is working the late shift. We are just walking and talking like other kids do. We even share a little about each other; she is not sure what happened to her mom and dad. They died when she was very young. She has no idea what they did at Girta. She didn't know they worked at Girta until Ming's mentioned the connection. Her uncle doesn't or won't talk about her parents, but then he doesn't talk about much, she says. Having lost his own wife to alcohol and drugs, his "ex" is still out there and floats back into his life from time to time whenever she needs something, like money.

She started chasing Ripfolds a few months ago, mainly out of boredom, a way to escape her day-to-day life. The first time she saw one she explains, "I just walked up and grabbed it." There's a shocker, I am thinking. "Of course, you did," I say out loud.

Since she mentioned Girta and Ming's, I want to talk to her about Mr. TC Singh, The Guru Nanak of Cincinnati, the warehouse on Wooster Pike, and, of course, Paul and Peter Huang. Wondering how to start the conversation, I bring out my phone, flip it open, and scroll to pictures. I bring up the Huang's and hand it to Jules. Again, Jules looks at me then smacks me hard in the shoulder.

"What?" I say, perplexed at my punishment. "I open up my personal life to you and the best you can do is show me a picture?" "Look closer." As I nod toward the phone she looks down, looks at me, looks back down. "I always wondered if he had a real name," she says." I thought someday he might just tell me."

In as few words as I can muster, I tell Jules about meeting TC at the gurdwara, dinner at his home, the warehouse, and the photo. As we are now approaching the diner, I lean across her to open door and without warning Jules smacks me again, my arm for her punching bag.

"How long have you known all this?" she screams.

Chapter Seven

"A compiler is used to convert high-level programming language code into machine language code. On the other hand, an assembler converts assembly level language code into machine language code. Both these terms are relevant in context of programing and memory execution."

The Frisch Big Boy restaurant is a Cincinnati tradition starting with the "Mainliner" almost eighty years ago, Cincinnati's first year-round drive through and the first "Big Boy" restaurant. The Mainliner is located on Wooster Pike Road in the Village of Fairfax, just on the edge of downtown Cincinnati. It so happens that the Girta warehouse is a stone's throw from the Mainliner, at least that's how it looks on Google maps. Mr. Singh emailed the address to me just a few days ago, indicating the building is about ten miles from where I am. I tell Jules I need to start working on my driver's license or recruit a friend. Jules's way ahead of me and thinking it's time to get Jimmy involved. Jimmy got his license a few months ago. I'm not sure he can have two people in the car as Ohio has rules about that kind of thing for novice drivers. However, TC did ask me to help him clear up the issue with the warehouse, and Jimmy would love to meet Jules, so it's probably a good time to do both.

Jimmy is not much for rules, typically makes his own. He is big and strong maybe powerful a better term. Looks more like a football player than basketball. He is also all about guitar all the time. Until he has a roundball in his hands. He is different for sure, but we are friends. All three of us piled into his mom's old two door sedan, Julia crammed into the back. It's a beautiful day, not a cloud but a big winter storm dragging its way east to hit tomorrow night, typical Cincinnati weather. Google is taking us to the warehouse then to

Mainliner for late lunch, Jimmy, Jules, and me. Jules decided last night it would be easier if Jimmy thinks of us as dating. She thinks it's self-explanatory and will keep Jimmy from probing too hard; no complaints from me. It is Thursday just after high noon. There's a teacher conference so half school day, but both Jimmy and I need to be back by six because tonight is the big rematch with Princeton, big for us at least. Princeton is still undefeated, still number one in the city, but we are at home. If we win, we join the conversation for best in town.

The three of us are getting acquainted with small talk as we head downtown. Jules tells Jimmy she knows of him by coming to our games, she knows he is our best defender. I am impressed; this compliment isn't lost on Jimmy either. She comes to our games I am thinking she never told me she came to our games. I don't know why this is such a surprise to me but kind of a cool surprise.

The warehouse isn't really on Wooster Pike but a small descending side road. There's no sign that I could see but following directions we take a right as Google directs and head toward the tree line behind the row of buildings. In the distant background there is highway traffic, like ants streaming busily above it all. On the right side of the little roadway there are two large warehouses with numerous trucks unloading. To the left another warehouse with a large parking field is closed and empty for now. As the road curls and ends, Google maps tells us we have arrived. There is an environmental services sign attached to a long pole in front of us. It appears the presumed Girta building is in two contiguous sections.

There are no Girta signs in site as the building structure is resting horizontal at the lower level of the tree line and overhead but distant highway. We see offices to the right for an environmental services business and a long warehouse building to the left. The warehouse portion is not very high, maybe fifteen feet with two roll-up doors for drive up, no dock high out front. The parking fields of the two surrounding structures combine so there's plenty of room to maneuver trucks and cargo with a goal to exit the same way you come in. A few cars are dispersed around the environmental services side to the right, but only one car is in front of the warehouse entrance next to a large dumpster. The door is maybe twenty feet from the last roll-up but all the way south or left of the warehouse building, the farthest point from the offices.

There are two things that strike me right away. There appear to be shadows, thin shadows, wisp-like clouds moving in and around the exterior walls and roof of the warehouse. Like a school of devil rays, the shadows appear to hover on the far-left side of the warehouse building. Strangely there are no clouds in the sky; these shadows moving like a tree sway. However, the tree line is well behind the building before it ascends toward the highway. No tree canopy or tree cover even close to the building. For the life of me I can't figure out where the shadows come from. It's early afternoon sun, like a basketball just off the shooting arch and now falling toward the rim to the west. By the look on Jules's face, she sees this too.

The other thing that grabs my attention is a large pile in and around the dumpster. We stopped the car in the parking field about thirty feet from the building. The pile looks like a cluster of boomerangs, one on top of another, yes, boomerangs, a bunch of boomerangs. I don't remember ever seeing one in my entire sixteen years in Cincinnati, much less a large pile of old discarded used boomerangs right in front of me.

As I am processing this, the warehouse door begins to open. Reflexively all three of us duck low in the car. Go figure. It's not like anyone is expecting us. In any event we do this simultaneously. In the meantime, out walks a young man, older than the three of us. As our heads slowly emerge over the dash, I can see his back is to us. I'm guessing he is turning the lock to the door. As the man swings around toward the car, Jules gasps. We see him, all three of us clearly see him. We know him well at least Jules and I know him. It's our Ming's, Peter Huang. Jimmy now looks right at both of us, not at Peter, and we are clearly shocked. He can tell by both of us slowly slinking down in our seats, now well below the window line. Jimmy is the only one visible. Jimmy, realizing he is the man on the outside looking in, says, "there is more going on here than meets the eye." We both nod at him from down under.

In short order Ming's is in the car and driving up the hill to Wooster Pike. Jules, still low in the back seat says, "follow him, lets follow him."

Jimmy always game, waits a moment then puts the car in drive and the chase is on but doesn't last long. All the way to the Mainliner one block away it appears we aren't the only ones who think it's lunchtime. Ming's has pulled into the Frisch's.

The Mainliner has a long parking field, and we pull in and immediately park to the right, Ming's now inside. Since we know our target is preoccupied, I want to go back and walk around the warehouse, get a decent look at the building and area, so back we go. Jimmy parks on the office side of the warehouse and we all get out, all of us wanting to get a closer look. Since we don't know how long we have before Ming's return, I ask Jimmy and Jules to circle around to the back as I want to get a closer look at the area around the dumpster. Walking over now and looking over the items I think of as boomerangs, they are not boomerangs, but they have the same look and shape. I bend over to pick one up. My hand passes right through them, not over them but right through them. I then try again, nothing. I can see these things, but I can't grab one. Normally this might freak me out, but at this point not much rattles my cage. Just for grins I stand up and try kicking them. Of course, my leg passes right through them, throws me off balance, and I spin landing on my butt. I remember the group of kids walking past me after my first Ripfold exit. "What a dork," I say out loud, mimicking the boys. Jimmy, having come around the corner now laughing having seen the entire episode, says, "got that right."

Jimmy tells me Jules is inside. The back door was not only unlocked, he says, but it was propped open, likely indicating Ming's doesn't expect to be gone long. He helps me up, I brush off the dirt and we jog quickly to the back. As we both walk in, I look at my phone. We probably have just a few minutes, so I ask Jimmy to pull out his phone and video everything to the right, and I take off to the left, doing the same thing. Jules is nowhere to be seen. I don't want to yell out her name. I am walking north in the warehouse toward the office portion. There are rows and rows of industrial shelving full of boxes and old equipment, just as Mr. Singh indicated. It feels a little like a maze. I count five rows of shelves each with three storage levels top to bottom. This shelving appears to extend at least to the clearing at the first external bay door. As I clear the shelving, I see Jules sitting at a long row of computers and other equipment placed along the front wall. There is a laptop open, but the screen is black. She is paging through a notebook. Sitting right next to the laptop is Binky's book, *For Whom the Bell Tolls*.

"What you got," I say in a low whisper as I come up next to her. She looks at me, smiles, jumps up, kisses me on the cheek and falls back into the chair.

"I think these are Ming's notes from your mom's book. I am guessing he is transferring them to the computer you see open," she says. I am a little off kilter from the kiss when we both hear Jimmy say, "Hey love birds, we need to get moving your man will be back soon." There are no windows so no easy way to know when he might return. Jules gets up, and we all walk quickly toward the back door. As we are stepping out, I hear keys at the front door,

"Go, go, go" I, say in shotgun whisper. "He is at the front door." We all kind of run into each other and start laughing as we fumble at the exit and wean out behind the building. As I move forward, I lose my balance a bit, trying not to plow into Jules, and my right-hand falls to the outside wall.

One of the shadows I saw earlier passes under it, yes clearly under it. The shadow passed under my hand. The virtual boomerangs didn't freak me out, but this does. Jules quickly sees what is happening, tries the same thing, and it happens to her. Jimmy watches us wondering what's up, so he leans over and puts both his hands on the wall, frisk me style.

"What are we doing guys?" he asks in a low tone.

"Good question," I respond." Let's get out of here."

We all pile back into the car with Jules and me again sinking low into the seats as Jimmy pulls out. As we are about to drive up the hill, I ask him to circle back to mid-parking field. I ask them both to look at the dumpster and tell me what they see. Jules sees a pile of something but can't quite tell what it is. Jimmy thinks she's batty.

"No wonder you two get along," he says, "There is nothing there, nothing at all."

Driving home, we are mostly silent not much choice. Jimmy loves extreme punk/metal, and we are listening to classic Thrash. Not sure if listening is right term way to loud to hear a thing. Just the way Jimmy likes it. Jules, however, wants to talk and pushes her leg out from the back seat. Hits the power button with big toe side of her right shoe. Quickly silence all around. She thinks Ming's might be living in the warehouse as she found a small bedroom area on the back wall between the two roll-up doors. Jules indicates she thinks Ming's might be living in the warehouse as she found a small bedroom area on the back wall between the two roll-up doors. Jimmy, upon hearing this, decides he has had enough for one day; he makes it clear, however, he expects a full download soon. Finally, I point out it's almost four thirty, and we need to be at the gym by six. Jules asks if she can grab a ride with us to the game, and I just smile. Jimmy then takes a quick look at both of us and starts shaking his head.

"I have a feeling this is the start of something big, but hell if I know what that might be."

When you can boomerang yourself through time, a simple high school basketball game might not seem like much, but we beat Princeton. Over the years I have been playing basketball, very few players, very few teams can say that. Princeton doesn't lose very often, maybe five times in five years, but we beat them soundly, by ten points. The press is going to play up my shooting and points, but truth is Jimmy won the game. Jimmy shut down their star, a true Division One prospect. The Princeton guard is on every college's radar, everyone is after him from Ohio State to Kansas. After him just like Jimmy was for four quarters, for all night and then shutting him down.

Jimmy, Jules, and I head out now, hours after the game. It feels good to be a high school kid, I am thinking as we pull into the Pizza Hut in Blue Ash; Pizza Hut is the after-game hangout for many of our students. The parking lot is full, the restaurant I am guessing even fuller with the game long behind us. But it still feels good, and we are now in conversation for best in town, best in Cincinnati, maybe one of the best in the State. Many of those here recognize us and give us loud welcome. These are our students, our crowd, our team. Just parking and getting out of the car was fun, many of those parked were screaming and yelling around us. As we entered the restaurant, I put my two hands on Jimmy's shoulders and push him forward for all to see.

The real star, I am thinking, we need to learn to enjoy these moments. In the span of a lifetime, they probably don't happen that often. I think of Claude and Mona, more importantly, I wonder how Jules feels. This is a Sycamore moment, and here she is, she is still a Loveland Tiger but quickly becoming part of us. I couldn't be happier. I'm not completely sure yet what makes her tick, but I'm not that worried. When the time comes, she will let me know. Let us know with emphasis on us, thinking to myself, meaning the three of us; Jimmy, Jules, and me. Maybe Ming's as well. I'm not ready to write him off yet. My instincts tell me Ming's is not a bad guy, maybe misdirected, who knows? If anyone can figure it out, we can. It's time to confront Ming's, I am thinking sooner rather than later, only fair to him and probably best for us.

Sports news a few days later still has Princeton number one. It happens; the writers not convinced the win was real, but we may see them again in the playoffs.

Jules and I have been texting this morning, talking about the game, Pizza Hut, and now Ming's. Julia thinks we should try to meet him at the Mainliner, let Ming's know we want to meet there, not at the Chinese Street Food diner, but the Frisch's Mainliner. He is very intelligent. She says he will know, and he will understand, he will know we discovered or uncovered Girta and the warehouse.

I couldn't agree more, but I text, "don't forget Jimmy, we need him to drive us, and he deserves to know what is going on."

Well, that will be an eye opener," Jules responds.

"Beginning of something big according to Jimmy," I text back then follow with, "we should let him absorb the conversation, no need for detail before the meeting."

"Not sure how Ming's will react. Jimmy's presence might cause him to clam-up, or retreat," is her response," "he can be a little intimidating," she ends. Please text him tell him all three of us are coming and let's see what happens."

Now it's the first Saturday after we raided the warehouse, and the three of us headed to the Mainliner. Ming's is already there when we arrive. He has a large booth in the corner to the very back, an older gentleman reading the *Wall Street Journal* a table or two away and a middle-aged Black couple in adjoining booth fixing to leave. Julia slips next to Ming's; Jimmy and I take the far seat with our backs to the wall facing the two of them. Ming's wastes no time jumps right in.

"So, it was the three of you in my place last week? I knew someone had been there, could feel it. I now recognize Jimmy from the car in the lot. I thought you were waiting for one of the young girls from the environmental services company." His voice is calm, controlled, he is not agitated, I am thinking.

"Oh well, doesn't really matter," Ming's continues." So, Brandon you have met with Mr. TC Singh, and you know about me and my dad."

Not really a question he has rehearsed or thought about how he wants to proceed. Without responding, I pull out my phone, move to pictures, scroll to the Huang's and push it forward. He nods, shakes his head up and down.

"Clearly you found my warehouse, my home, it has been many years since my dad died and I have been here in this area and this building ever since. Upwards of ten years now, I have spent much of that time trying to recreate the work he started and possibly take it to the next level. I still I believe I can. Having said that you, Julia, and Binky's notes helped me come a long way. I learned more in the last few months than I did since I started. I am not one of you," he says, Jimmy is now paying attention "I don't have your power or gift." Looking at me and Jules, he added, "As I mentioned to you before, I cannot see or enter one of the Ripfolds. I do, however, understand to some degree now what happened at Girta.

"You should know I probably caused Jeeves to disappear. I used him to try and understand how the Assemblers and Compilers work. At the time I didn't know what might happen. How could I? But even if I did, I would likely not have changed my focus or more importantly the outcome. Then I started to do the same thing with you. Brandon, when you appeared on the scene, I thought you might be the link to take me to the next level. However, it didn't take me long to realize you are different, clearly different. Jeeves didn't care about anyone but himself, but you are different."

"I could have told you that," Jimmy says, jumping in and trying to break the one-way street of conversation coming from Ming's.

"Jimmy, Peter, Ming's," Huang says out loud, looking right at him, "you don't know about our two friends here. I can tell both Brandon and Jules are different, more different than you can possibly imagine, gifted maybe rather than different, not because they want to be, but because they are," he says with emphasis. "They were born that way. I have learned a little about what they are and what happened, and I spent the last ten years trying to become like them, maybe even one of them. It might help me find my dad. My dad and I worked at the same company both Brandon and Julia's parents worked; Girta Technologies. Both Brandon and Julia are infected with a virus that cannot live outside of their bodies. According to my father's and Binky's notes, it cannot be transmitted and thrives solely and exclusively for Brandon and Julia or those who might be like them, Jeeves, for example. Binky believed direct offspring and only direct offspring would be infected and any further spread was stopped and buried by either the parents and/or Girta. She knew however, knew this might be wishful thinking. Viruses are tricky, they can change, mutate, and evolve and they seem to do this randomly without apparent cause. Viral work is known to be unpredictable. We have talked about this before, don't forget the Olaf, Ripfold trip, you did not connect the memory you made him forget the memory.

Your mother's notes were clear on one point, Brandon. She knew you would be infected. She knew this infection would impact your life but probably did not know the extent of the impact thus, the reason *For Whom the Bell Tolls*. It is written by her primarily, to get the message to her only son and to warn you. She also knew something else; if the government found out about you and the others, they would have stepped in. They would have acted against you and the others. I believe this is the primary reason she artfully hid her work. The intimacy of her work is not contained in these notes. The notes a part of *For Whom the Bell Tolls* appear to be more a warning or wake up call for you," Ming's finishes.

Julia jumps in, "Ming's," she says, "your dad worked at the Girta lab. Logically you should also be infected."

"I thought so at first but remember my dad and I came later after the two companies merged. In fact, by the time we arrived, Girta had shifted its focus from the viral research for the NIH to the possible medical or therapeutic application of manipulating messenger

RNA." Ming's says. "This pathway is the one my dad took when he started working at the Girta central location. I have continued this work for the last many years, still my primary focus as I have licensed some of the intellectual property my dad patented. It is how I survive and pay the bills," he continues. "Binky's notes, on the other hand, are focused on the early work meant specifically, I believe, to give Brandon the background and detail he needs to deal with the virus in his body and the changes in his life. She likely did not know what that would be. How could she? It is possible, I guess, that she was like the two of you that she herself was infected. Maybe she could also enter and influence and change memory in the Ripfold. This possibility is also missing from her notes."

Ming's falls silent as we all do. Now what, where do we go from here, I am thinking while we sit in silence, noticing that the Black couple is now gone but the older gentleman reading the *Wall Street Journal* is still there. He hasn't turned a page in quite some time, must be one good investment tip, I am thinking. I decided to keep conversation going with Ming's.

"The warehouse Ming's, and the computers along the wall, are these the Assemblers we have discussed?" I ask in a much lower tone than before.

"I don't really know," he responds with matching hush, acknowledging to me he sees the gentleman to the left of Jimmy. "I think they may be but really have no way of knowing. They are not labeled as such, so there is not enough information available to me to make that call."

"You mentioned Jeeves and using him to understand the Assemblers. Did you learn anything?" I ask.

"Jeeves was openly exposing himself by going back and forth in the Ripfolds. The Assemblers seemed to learn more and more about his physical presence, his real-world presence. We assumed the Assemblers had no real clue on how this might be happening. This is all theory, no proof, it's not like the computers in the warehouse turn on from time to time or start to heat up when one of you enter a Ripfold. They are always on. I have slept near them for almost a decade, hoping something would become obvious, apparent. No such luck. We have talked about this before at the Street Food Diner. We know from the Girta work that the, Assemblers and Combiners were specifically programmed to find and destroy the virus, and we have assumed everything that is a part of it. Remember I knew what I was asking him to do was exposing him, dangerous for sure, but I did not know what might occur. Of course, I was not expecting the outcome to be good. I will say one thing, Jeeves kept talking about how he was changing, his old self, 'vanishing,' he used to say. This, however, was not physically apparent, not apparent to me and not obvious from the photo record. Impossible to know if this was mental, physical, or even psychosomatic for him, but eventually Jeeves did seem to disappear. He just wasn't there anymore," Ming's recalls. "As I told you before, to this day we don't know; if he moved, if the US secret forces dragged him away or if he just disappeared, vanished."

Jules jumping in, asking if Jeeves or Ming's kept a log or record of what was happening.

"Yes," Ming's says, maintaining the hushed tone. "I kept a full log and photo history, but I don't think you will learn much from scrutinizing it. But you are welcome to try," he indicates, happy to email."

"Might be better to keep where it is for now?" I whisper, acknowledging the *Wall Street Journal* man a few feet away. No one else at our table was apparently aware of his presence.

My head is spinning a bit. Ming's seems genuine and I remember he can't see the Ripfolds. I assume that also means he can't see the devil ray-like shadows or whisps hovering and moving over the warehouse roof. Almost certainly he can't see the pile of "boomerangs" sitting right in front of him, next to the dumpster, next to his car. I remember without mentioning to the others my virtual foot problem a couple of weeks ago, maybe the work of the Assemblers, maybe my imagination. My foot is now back in one large visible piece. Fortunately for me, all my extremities are now present and accounted for. This thought reminds me I did not video the devil ray-like shadows on the warehouse, nor did I video the boomerang heap, so I make a mental note to return to the warehouse and do both. My lone thought because I have not discussed with the group, is we need to try and uncover the person that is Jeeves. Sounds like Ming's may have information or history that we can work with. Jeeves is one of us, and we need to at least try to find him. This effort might lead to something good, maybe even something extraordinary. I also need to find out what Jules, Jimmy, and Ming's think. How hard can it be, I am thinking.

Enough for now we are headed out and away from the Mainliner, back to Evandale and back to our side of town. We agreed to meet Ming's in a week at the warehouse. He will download us then on anything new. On the way home, I can sense Jimmy has a few questions, so I volunteer and jump in.

"Look Jimmy," I say. "I realize that some of the conversation with Ming's might have come across a little strange. Well, it is strange. What Jules and I have been experiencing is more than a little strange. I haven't tried to explain this to anyone, what has been going on with us, at least not to anyone outside Jules, Ming's, and myself, so you will be the first," I say.

"Lucky me," he responds.

"Yeah right," I say. "You may recall a while back we were walking to the gym with the guys, and I mentioned to you and the boys I was seeing cuts or rips in the sky and wondered out loud if you and the others might see them."

"I remember making a lude comment," Jimmy jumps in, "which I won't repeat for Jules's presence."

"Yep, much appreciated," I say. "Well, it turns out the cuts or rips are real, they exist. As far as we know only Jules and I can see them, but bear with me," I say to Jimmy with emphasis, "because that's not the strange part. So, this is where it gets a little funky, more than a little weird. We can go into one, we can enter one of the Ripfolds, as we now call them. Jules once described these as actual cuts or open wounds. I tend to think of them like that, like wounds. When we grab one, we get thrown into another time, another place and when we arrive, we are programmed to perform a job, to assist someone. To assist them to remember to do something, something they forgot, but very important to them to help mend a wound, a wound in time, a wound in their memory, left open because a virus made them forget."

Jimmy is smiling now, trying to follow the conversation but clearly thinking I am over the top.

"One more thing," I add. "Before you say anything, as soon as we mend the wound, the very moment we help make the connection, we are boomeranged out of the Ripfold back to where we started, no worse for wear."

Nothing for a bit, Jimmy just drives. still looking forward to the road.

"When you jump into these wound things, the Ripfolds," Jimmy says, "do you eat?"

"What?" I respond slightly aggravated, "No, we don't eat, we are busy," I say somewhat loudly." We are changing lives," I say.

"Well, can we?" he screams back, "because I am fricking starving."

"Thought you would never ask," screams Jules from the back seat. We spot a Wendy's Hamburger restaurant, Jimmy's hand quickly to the volume control as the three of us along with Motorhead exit the highway laughing, singing and rolling like a bunch of crazy teenagers.

Chapter Eight

"A computer's CPU manages and coordinates the device, getting instruction from the memory. The CPU, once receiving the memory instruction, then interprets and directs the operation."

"I have been thinking about what the two of you told me at the restaurant last week and put a few thoughts together. Some real gray matter to it," Jimmy is saying as we drive to meet Ming's at the warehouse. He is panning between me, Julia, and the road as he speaks. It's been about a week since the confrontation with Ming's at Frisch's, and Jimmy is on a roll.

"Ever since we hit Wendy's coming back from the Mainliner when you played out the whole Ripfold thing for me," he says again, "I've been working it over and over in my mind. Of course, I have always known someday I would help make Branded a star. In fairness to me, I was thinking earth bound kind of stuff; you know college, NBA, big contract, maybe movies.

"This is bigger, bigger than any of that okay, okay enough. I am sure you two get that so, listen to this," he says with emphasis. "We need some branding. We need an image, something to take it up a notch. Now don't say anything until I finish, let what I have to say sink in, drum roll please." Then he begins. "The dynamic duo, meaning the two of you," he says, head still panning, "with Memory Man, right, right because Branded here, you're the memory guy, and Julia as the data base, for Julia play off database with Data Babe! Because you, Julia, do the database and programming and Data Babe because it's catchy, introducing the dynamic duo of Memory Man and Data Babe," he concludes with great enthusiasm. "Then we throw in Ming's, the Mad Scientist and Jimmy 'the Greek'

Wadsworth, trusted agent, and advisor." Finally, silence as it all sinks in with Jules and me.

This is pure Jimmy, I am thinking. Jimmy might be intimidating even aggressive to some, but to me he has a musician's heart, though this is probably not his best work.

"The Greek," I say to Jimmy breaking the silence. "Where did that come from?"

"Toyed with Jimmy 'Wah Wah' Wadsworth," he says, "but thought we need better, more class." Wah Wah is Jimmy's nickname amongst the boys. Because the only thing in his hand more often than a basketball is a guitar. Jules, now staring, glaring right through the rearview mirror right at Jimmy, "Don't you ever (emphasis on ever) call me data babe," she says with authority.

"I get it, I get it," Jimmy jumps in already back stroking." I wanted to see how you might react, but I have some other ideas." Jimmy is now in full retreat. Silence, then Jimmy back on stage ..." the dynamic duo of Memory Man and Cache, Cache as in C A C H E." He spells out the word with each letter, like stacks or storage. Cache, simple, kind of sexy and still follows the theme?" As Jimmy leaves this thought hanging for Jules to absorb.

"Well follows or following as the theme is spot on," Jules says mildly amused, "because I think that man driving the silver Lexus a couple cars behind might be following us," Julia says. This causes Jimmy and I to look behind at the oncoming traffic, Jimmy, his eyes now wide and staring right at Jules in the rearview mirror.

"What, Jimmy," Jules asks, somewhat annoyed. "Why are you staring at me?"

"Was that some sort of superpower you have?" he asks, "because I can barely tell that the car is silver much less that it's a Lexus and there is man driving."

"Grow up," she responds." Same car, same man from the Mainliner last week, the one reading the WSJ. I memorized his car and plate while we were leaving," Jules says, winking at me. Now I am the one thinking she has superpowers. I didn't even know the WSJ man registered with her. Cache is way out front I better watch my step around her, I am thinking, a warm smile from me to return the wink.

"Jimmy, can you slowly work over to the far-right lane to exit? Let's see if Wall Street Journal man follows," I suggest.

"I like that," he says, "the Wall Street Journal Man. Our first real life villain," he says, now smiling and right turn signal blinking. We exit and now halfway up the long winding turn lane, sure enough the Lexus in tow. Jules spots an IHOP sign on the corner off the exit. "Jump into the IHOP, maybe he will want to join us?" Jules suggests.

Seat yourself, the sign reads as we enter, so we grab a booth along the window and wait. Jimmy and Jules have their backs to the door as I suggest. Jules is texting Ming's, let him know we might be a little late. She is already on it and a few minutes later guess who walks in. I watch the WSJ man come inside. He doesn't look ominous or aggressive, well dressed, groomed and aware, medium height, slim with silver hair. He is now coming down our aisle and I am debating whether to stand and see if he wants to join.

He beats me to the punch. Walking up to our table, he looks politely and nods at Jules, Jimmy then to me." Brandon," he says holding out his hand, "Robert Alcott. President of Girta when your mother Binky was a part of the team." I attempt to squeeze out of the booth, now trying awkwardly to stand up next to him. Then half in, half out of seat, I somewhat clumsily extended my own hand as we shake hands. I can feel he is sizing me up.

"Well," he says now looking up at me. "You are clearly no longer seven years old. May I join you guys?" he asks. I scoot back into the booth and held out my right hand to invite him to sit. He slides right behind me and begins to introduce himself more formally to Jules and Jimmy.

"First, I apologize for sneaking up on you guys. A little creepy. I know, an explanation is in order. My wife and I live in Montgomery, we like Ming's diner. A couple of weeks ago I walked in to pick up our order and saw you and Peter Huang. Saw the three of you," now nodding to Julia, "sitting in the diner. I only knew you, Brandon, from the basketball pictures in the newspaper. I saw an article about you late last year and figured you were Binky's son by the looks and last name. Started watching the news for articles about you in the weekend sports page as you are now a regular feature.

"Jimmy," as Alcott turns to look at him, "I recently saw you highlighted after the Princeton win. Congrats to both of you. Good win for the Loveland program," he says." I didn't really confirm it was Peter until I left Ming's that night, looking back through the window. I must admit this opened a flood gate of questions for me, seeing Binky's and Paul Huang's sons together. Full confession, I then followed you last week when you headed downtown. That's the creepy part, except of course for today, also creepy and unprofessional. Last week I lost you around the Wooster Pike cut off from I-75 and went to the Mainliner out of frustration to eat. That was the location of the first real date with my wife. You can imagine my surprise when Peter then the three of you walk in, even more so when you sat nearby. Again, sorry my actions were uncalled for and clearly a little weird." His body language indicates he is finished.

"Thanks for that explanation," I say. That helps at least for me but, why? Why was it weird for you to see Peter and I together?" I ask, "What's weird enough about the two of us together, weird enough for you to spend your day tracking and following us?" I add.

"Well, that's the million-dollar question I guess," he says. "In truth was hoping you might tell me." He stops and looks at the three of us, then continues. "Binky and Paul were the Girta company's lead scientists. Eventually your friend Peter got in the thick of things as well. Binky's early work was extremely sensitive, but when the Huang's joined, things got out of hand. Very dicey, Huang manipulated Binky's research into a different direction, significantly different objectives. Your mother, Binky, fought the changes. Paul and then Peter bullied forward but the combination left me with no choice but to shut down the program. However, there were unanticipated repercussions, strange things happened, things you might not believe if I told you. We spent millions trying to contain the impact to the program, the impact to Girta and most importantly to our people.

"Eventually we received funding to gear the research in a different direction and things settled down. I'm not being melodramatic when I say this action saved the company then TC and I sold a few years later," he says.

"In all honesty, full disclosure, I was wondering," now asking, looking directly at me, "if you might be experiencing anything out of the ordinary, anything different or strange?" Before I can answer the question, Jules decides to change the conversation. Clearly my body language says enough.

"Mr. Alcott," she says, "would you happen to remember my parents, Don and Joanna Childs? They both worked for Girta about the same time as Brandon's mom." This question grabs Robert's full attention. Now there's a third Girta participant in the mix for him to consider. You can almost feel him thinking. He turns from looking directly at me to Julia.

"Don and Joanna Childs? You're Julia Childs, then correct? He repeats. "No, I do not recall those names," he says out loud.

"However, I have access to old records and can look them up, let you know what I find."

Jimmy now jumps in." Well, you might be glad to know, Mr. Alcott, my parents work at P&G and are still happily employed." This causes Robert to smile, helps all four of us to relax. Jimmy also reminds us Ming's is waiting.

"He means Peter, Peter Haung" I say to Mr. Alcott. "We call him Ming's." Robert is again smiling, probably remembering, we are only kids.

"How about this?" he says. "I promise to leave you alone and promise to research Julia's parents' information.

"When and if you are ready, let's get together, this time because you want to. There are many ways I can help if help is needed, many ways," he says with emphasis. As he says this, he pushes a business card out to each of us and stands up. "I enjoyed meeting you and hope to see you again soon." Then he walks off.

The three of us are now back in the car, ready to go to, the warehouse and meet with Ming's. Jimmy can't resist. He starts the car but leaves it in park and turns to look at us.

"Memory Man, Cache, and Jimmy the Greek slam dunkin' the WSJ Man, not bad for our first super-hero battle," he says as he turns to high five Jules then me as we are laughing and enjoying this together.

A couple of weeks later March has begun and it's cold, bitter cold. Jules and I are now at the Findlay Market in the heart of downtown Cincinnati. Findlay Market is the last Ripfold sighting given by Jeeves to Ming's. Nothing is clearly visible, no fold currently in sight. Ming's is reluctant to cooperate after we told him about Alcott. Clearly there is no love lost between the two. According to Ming's, Jeeves did bike deliveries for Eckerlin Meats, a well-known butcher at the Findlay, well known for their goetta.

Goetta is breakfast meat, but most people don't think it's meat, more like cereal and pork puttied together then pan fried. Remember now my mom used to make eggs, goetta, and toast for me, typically on weekends remembering now how she would reminisce while we ate. I never eat it anymore.

We are making our way to Eckerlin, walking outside along the outer perimeter of the Market. Jimmy drops us off and circles to park the car. There is no practice tonight; this is our first break from basketball in a long time. Playoffs start next week, and it feels good to get a break, although it is cold, enjoying the time and walk with Jules. We both see and comment on the large gray rats painted, and stacked one on top the other, each one smaller than the last now enshrined on the upper half outside wall to the far right. These buildings create a nice walkable area with shops and cafés facing the market stalls along the Essen Strasse. Apartments above, I'm guessing chock full of budding couples and future families, very cool. As we bring our focus back to Findlay, I see it, almost step in it, the Ripfold. This one is on the ground just off an outside table, one of Findlay restaurant's tables close to the side entrance into the market. This fold is small, dim, and partially buried. I don't think I have ever seen a Ripfold partially buried in the ground before. It kind of looks like it is being sucked into the dirt. I might have stepped into it but for bumping into Jules, both of us seeing it about the same time.

Learning from Ming's lecturing and our first Ripfold journey, together we decide Jules should go first. As always, without hesitation, she sticks her left foot out and Bang, she is gone. I have no idea how long I should wait before following, but it feels awkward standing here. It's cold and I am uncomfortable that Jules is inside without me.

I decided to move forward and get closer to the fold. As I do, a shadow passes over the entire area, then a cold chill, then colder still. I look around as if a breeze or bluster has blown in but see nothing. I put my foot out to stand on the fold, but as my foot approaches, I feel it hit me. It hits hard like I am being trampled now, tackled without warning, feeling like I have been slammed right into the Ripfold and Bang we are gone. I lay stunned on the ground inside the fold.

"We are still at Findlay Market," I say. We because I mean she and I. I am staring up at a little girl, she is staring right back at me with astonishment in her eyes. I don't think I can move and feel like I am pinned down but almost as soon as I am aware of this, something pushes off from me, and I don't see anything but a wiry shadow. It's really nothing but it felt strong and determined, whatever it is or was gone now and went straight for the girl.

It's warm outside, almost dusk. Findlay is crowded with people in all directions. Clearly, I am in the Ripfold and still on the ground. I know this little girl is the reason I am here. I know this but I am outside of her, not inside where I belong. I am supposed to be inside, and don't have a clue what to do. Whatever slammed into me, whatever pushed off from me, attempted to pass through her and might be inside of her now, maybe to take my place. I have a very bad feeling there is something terribly wrong. Then panic hits,

"Jules," I yell. Jules is still inside her, but before I can move a single muscle, I feel my body being sucked back to the Ripfold. Soon after, less than a second, I'm thrown out of the fold like discarded rubbish or garbage hitting the hard ground.

We are both now on our butts, Jules and I, both sprawled on the ground, landing next to the table where we saw the Ripfold. Back to where we started. We are both clearly shaken. I feel like I was hit by a truck. Jules is now sitting up but crying, trying to talk, and I crawl over to put my arm around her. We just sit there for a few minutes.

"When I saw you on the ground next to me inside the fold I panicked," she says. "I was inside the little girl, Mae, we were looking right at you, she was eleven. We were there to help her remember. Since you were outside of her, I reacted on pure instinct. I reversed my attempt to install memory in Mae. This action, I think, moved everything in reverse, everything back a few seconds in time. This sent you out of the Ripfold and I followed." Now Jules looks right at me. "Something else there was someone else inside of Mae with me. I could feel it, felt cold, desperate maybe sick."

We just sat for a while, recovering. "Whatever or whoever it was, it was not you, I know that" Jules says. "I know something else, I know the memory," she tries to say." I know what memory we were to restore," she says, dropping her head and starting to cry again. "We were reminding the little girl, Mae, she already had the candy money," Jules says. "She was going back to ask her mom for candy money. Her mom was outside at a table. Mae forgot it was already in her pocket." As Jules says this, she opens her hand, and two or three wadded up dollar bills fall from her palm onto the ground.

"Then the shooting started. Mae ran right in front of it. Mae should have been inside the market when the shooting started, buying gum," she finishes.

I see it before Jules does, there are two hands, one further along than the other. The right hand has the base of the restaurant table; the left hand is gripping a leg. Some tables at Findlay are nailed to the perch to battle the Cincinnati wind. Jules sees it now. This thing, this person is coming from inside the Ripfold, also shooting out of the fold, a light or a strobe. The whole scene, the Ripfold, the grasping hands, table, and light make the scene look like the earliest of motion picture film, white and black shadows constantly flicking as each frame and movement occurs and only seconds have passed. Then, without warning, the Fold begins to move. It startles us and we both scamper reverse crab-like up the small hill to get further away. It's collapsing on itself, the crawler's head and torso briefly visible, now disappearing. Arms and hands free of the table quickly follow, and it's now completely gone with little or no struggle except for a scream of anguish and pain like being sucked up by a powerful vacuum from behind. Now everything outside is in, nothing left but an empty table. The fold is gone, vanished. It is silent as we sit stunned. Mae and her Ripfold are gone.

As Jimmy approaches, he can see something is wrong. He can see Jules now lightly crying. My arm is back around her shoulders. Jimmy takes a seat at the table. We are still on the ground, all of us silent, the severe cold now creeping up on us. Finally, Jules decides to get up. I followed, now looking at Jimmy.

"Let's get out of here," I say." Where did you park?"

Jimmy pops up. "Follow me," he commands but then almost immediately stops, bends, and picks up the wadded bills.

Look at that," he says, "it's my lucky day." We then walk out of Findlay Market together. We are just about to get into the car, and I am holding the door open for Jules. The look on her face says it all as she is staring at my feet. I look down, sure enough part of my right foot is gone again, nothing there but darkness.

In the wee hours of the next morning,

Jules? I text,

"Yes," almost instantly.

"That was scary," is all I say.

"Yea agreed," is her simple reply. More than a few minutes later I text, "If you had not reversed the memory, I would have been trapped in the Ripfold when it closed."

"I know," she responds. "Now what, I'm lost as to what to do next?"

"Do we have a choice?" is Jules's immediate answer.

"Assemblers clearly know you exist," alluding to my disappearing foot. "If Ming's is right, they now have clearer picture of me."

"Maybe if we quit now, walk away now, we can still go back to being teenagers?" I text.

Her response, "If we had fulfilled the memory, Mae would still be alive."

Not much more to say, I am thinking but these Ripfold trips are getting more and more dangerous as I drift off to sleep.

The next morning, I am up bright and early and send Jules a text.

"We need to go to Columbus." A few minutes later, "why?" is her ask. "We need to see if Ripfolds exist elsewhere, we need to know," I text back. "Road trip," is her only reply.

Chapter Nine

"A Compiler is computer software that compiles or translates source codes written in high-level language into a set of machine language instructions that can be understood by a machine's CPU. The computer CPU provides the instruction enabling the computer to do its work."

I'm lying in my bed at home waiting for Jimmy, then it's to team bus at 6:30 and our first playoff game. I realize now the Ripfold world can be dangerous. It's no longer a question. Whatever hit and tackled me at Findlay was real, whatever was inside of me and Mae was desperate. Body parts don't just fade away, they don't just go dark. Jeeves disappeared, am I now following in his footsteps? That makes me laugh, thinking about my foot. According to Ming's he was a Loader, like me. The darkness, a part of my foot could spread, then what? Who can we turn to for guidance? No, I'm not sure about Ming's, no clue about Robert Alcott, and Mr. TC Singh, not an option. Jimmy is already part of us, Ron and Agnes are out of the question. Then it hits me: how did Ming's know Jeeves was a Loader? How did Ming's know about Jules? He labeled her a Linker, programmed after the Assemblers were created. It's not like there is an instruction manual out there, or is there? How did he know? Were there others before Jeeves? There must be a trail there and might have been others. I recall Ming's comment, "There were over 100 people working for Girta, there are likely other kids like you, it stands to reason," he said.

I send Jules a text in the afternoon.

"We need to circle up with Ming's, after Findlay we need someone, we can trust our only choices, Ming's, or Robert Alcott we don't know enough about Alcott so all roads lead to Ming's."

A couple of days later, the best laid plans in life are clearly meant to change. I don't check my email very often, but Jimmy texts me to let me know coach sent out an email last night. We were upset in the first round of playoffs. The coach is probably venting. It's understandable. We were expected to make a deep run maybe even rematch Princeton in large school City finals. Since I rarely check my email, I'm glad Jimmy prompted me about coach's email. That's when I noticed another email this one from Robert Alcott.

"Sorry for the Deerfield loss, sure you expected better, but you are only a sophomore, many opportunities in front of you. I have information about Julia's mother. Let's get together," the email says. As I said, the best laid plan's are meant to change. Now maybe we work both fronts, Ming's and Alcott. I copy Alcott's email and text it to Jules. This is very important to her. I don't think she knows much about her mom.

Saturday late afternoon a few days after our loss to Deerfield, the three of us are at Ming's Chinese Street Food diner, Jules, me, and Alcott here for dinner, his treat. Since coming to the diner to eat Jules and I have grown very fond of ramen. Ramen is now right at the top right for me, right next to a cheeseburger and fries. Ramen is a Japanese noodle dish but served Chinese style in piping hot broth growing more and more popular in America. Our own international cuisine. Diane, our motherly waitress, comes over to the table as is typical, but this time looking a little confused. Alcott is clearly not Ming's.

"Well good to see you two again," she says, looking right at Jules and me. She thinks we are dating, and I of course hope she is right. "Mr. Alcott," Diane says, now looking at Robert, "nice to have you eating inside, welcome," he continues with friendly emphasis.

"Thanks Diane, I need to do this more often. Whatever they want it's on me," he says. She takes our order for drinks, food, and moves on.

"Guys, thanks for getting together and meeting with me. I am sure after my bungled surveillance maneuvers, I'm not high on your priority list. In any event I hope to change that tonight and start over. So, digging right in Julia, I knew your mother quite well. The name didn't click because I didn't know her as Joanna Childs. When I worked with her, we called her Anna. The team often referred to her as Anna Banana out of pure love for her, and I mean that sincerely. The nickname may sound derogatory. Believe me when I say it was anything but. However, Anna didn't work for Girta. We relied on her to supply us with animals needed for our viral research work. She supplied us with mice, hamsters, and more importantly primates or monkeys. These were needed, required really to carry out the NIH mission, hence the Anna Banana. I think the company she worked for still supplies The Ohio State University Infectious Disease Institute in Columbus.

"I can honestly say everyone loved her; she lit up a room. It's not easy to light up a room full of research scientists, but she could and did. I will confess to you when Anna was around, I found excuses to leave the confines of my office just to see her." Robert now looks directly at Jules. "You have many of her qualities," he says. "She had a way of making each person she met feel special. As a business owner I know this to be a rare and valuable trait."

I can tell Robert is earnest; he is genuinely happy about his relationship with Anna. He speaks from the heart and Jules is a loss for words. Me too.

The food arrives, and it's going to get cold; I can tell. Once Diana leaves Robert continues, "I could go on about Anna but there is another side to the story. She was as loving to the animals as she was to us. Some of the animals that survived, she kept. She knew this was dangerous, especially with the primates, and also illegal, remember they were subject to viral and genetic testing. Many were prone to violence, often sick, and the required protocol was to euthanize all animals injected or tested, no exceptions. She tried for a while to keep them on a small farm near Milford. I was not supposed to know this.

"Eventually, word got out, and the township chased them off. In addition, NIH caught up with her and the company lost their license for a bit, so we had to sever ties. In any event, soon thereafter she left the area, and I heard rumor she took some of the animals to a remote area outside Columbus. Eventually, word filtered down she fell sick and passed. Of course, this was all many years ago." He falls silent, not much else to say, I am thinking.

Eventually we all started to eat. Jules asks Robert about himself and family." I've been in the Ohio Valley a long time," he starts." I've been married to my wife even longer. I was lucky enough to pick the right person the first time around, not easy to do. We have two children. A son living in South Texas, in San Antonio, he has a good heart and people know and sense this about him. He's just starting his life's journey. I have a daughter here in Cincinnati, the love of my life, she took a life's tumble in her teenage years, but she's catching up fast now. I'm lucky enough to spend every other Saturday with her, mostly rummaging around town for hidden restaurant gems. Ming's was one of our early targets, and we've been coming here ever since. For me, I consult now and teach as an adjunct at UC, keeping busy even for an old guy."

We finished eating and were getting ready to leave while waiting for Diane to bring the final bill.

"Before I forget," Robert says, addressing Julia, "if you would like, I feel confident we can find specifics concerning your mom. If this is of interest to you just let me know.

"Also, Brandon, we should get together soon and discuss your mom. I worked very closely with Binky; she was my chief scientist and a friend." This, I think, will help open up the conversation between you and me. "Now between you, me, and Julia," he says as he pans to look at each of us.

"One thing you should know about Binky she was always certain, certain she was right, certain of her path, certain what to do next and why. What the two of you and possibly Peter is experiencing, I feel certain Binky knew it would happen, let's leave it at that."

We are all standing now. Alcott turning to leave, taking a few steps toward the door. Jules and I are both out of and next to the booth watching him leave when I hear Jules say, "Mr. Alcott." He turns and she almost immediately runs and falls into him with a deep hug. He is taken back at first but returns the embrace, and they stand that way for some time before Jules lets go, now speaking to his chest, "Before tonight I knew nothing about my mom, nothing at all, now it is so different. I don't know what else to say, thank you, thank you so much." We are all sobbing; Mr. Alcott can't speak or respond. Even Diane is tearing. Time for everyone to go home.

The four of us are now in the parking field facing the old Girta warehouse. Its Saturday, midday no basketball for a very long time. Spring break is in a week or so, and we have not heard from Alcott since our dinner. I was not planning to bring him up to the group today. The weather is still cold, but right now not so much. Jules and I talked yesterday, and both think it would be good to download Ming's and Jimmy, get them both focused on things they might not be aware of, things we see others may not.

This is the reason we are here today. We all need each other if this team is to be a success. Of course, there's no clue yet what success for us might look like.

The warehouse parking field is empty, it's the weekend. I ask Jimmy to park some distance from the building for a reason. We need a direct view of the entire structure. All four of us are standing mid-ship and facing the building. Jules and I both took a minute to look at the shadows moving along the exterior and roof. It reminds me of the scene in *A Christmas Carol* by Charles Dickens, where Ebenezer jumps out the window holding the cloak of the ghost of Christmas present. The sky is full of other ghosts, floating and circling around London town in the early morning. I start out describing to Ming's and Jimmy about the shadows running along the side walls and rooftop now pointing in that direction.

"Like a school of devil rays," I say out loud. "Maybe ten to fifteen but hard to tell because they circulate or flow constantly. I doubt they ever stop," I explain. "I believe they are only visible to Jules and me, maybe only those infected with the virus, although I have no way of knowing this for sure," I say and finish.

Now we begin walking toward the building, our small group follow, then in and around to the back, taking our time. There is no reason to hurry. As we approached the rear door, I remind Jimmy of when we were all leaning against the back wall on our first uninvited visit here. He was in mock arrest mode as he leaned against the structure, we were all attempting to avoid being discovered by Ming's as he returned from lunch. It was then one of the rays or shadows passed under my hand, I say out loud. Place my right hand on the wall for emphasis, "It was going under my hand rather than over my hand like you would expect of a typical shadow," I tell everyone. "This helped convince me these were something different, something other than natural shadows from cloud, birds, or surrounding trees." The hard part of this conversation is that only Jules and I can see these moving shadows. Jimmy and Ming's must accept what we tell them. Ming's silent but taking it all in.

We then circle around to the front again because I want to show the team the pile of boomerangs.

"I know this is getting weird. I also realize you can't see either the floating rays or this pile of trash in front of me. Right here next to the dumpster, to Jules and me, there is a pile of junk." I point to the spot on the ground for emphasis." To us it looks like a large pile of old boomerangs, not really boomerangs, they only resemble them. There are maybe 40 or 50 of these in the stack," I say guessing." To add to the weirdness, Jules and I can see them probably because we have the virus; however, we cannot physically pick them up.

That's right," I say again. "We can see them, but they have no physical substance." As I say this, I crouch down and pass my hand right through the pile. The pile that only Jules and I can see, the pile that is not there and I do not know why.

From here we go inside to get warm, now moving toward the row of computers assembled along the front wall. Ming's and Jules take a seat, Jimmy and I standing. Jules starts by unloading to the group what happened at Findlay Market as she and Mae were the only real witnesses. What she has to say is unusual enough for Ming's absolute science fiction for Jimmy. I then describe what happened to me before entering the Ripfold; the large shadow passing over, being tackled, and thrown inside, then the struggle with whatever "it" was that took me down, feeling it push off from me and appearing to join Jules inside of Mae. I describe the brief emergence of the Crawler, the strobe or flashing light, and the Ripfold closing in on itself like a black hole.

Finally, I pull up a chair and take off my right shoe "Ming's" I say, "and Jimmy," looking back and forth to both, "I know you can't really see this, however, my little toe and its neighbor, as well as a chunk of the middle foot behind them are not there. Jules and I can't see them. To us there's only a dark shadow, like someone has taken a magic marker and colored that part of my foot deep black. I can feel that these parts are there." I lean over and grab the right side of my foot, "but visibly just darkness. Ming's, you may recall the photos of Jeeves you shared with us on our last visit to you, Jules, and I. Everything appeared normal. Jeeves was all there in one piece, appearing normal in the photos, even though he was telling you he was vanishing. He kept telling you he was disappearing." Then I pull out my own phone and click to photos and scroll to the picture I took in my bedroom of my missing foot.

"The photos still show everything normal," I point out, "however, in person, live, Jules and I see nothing. Jeeves may have been much further along, and the darkness may have spread on him. You could not know this it would not have been visible to your eye nor in the photo history," The good news for me is that the darkness has not spread. In fact, recently from time to time I see a light outline of my foot again. Like it is trying to re-emerge. It kind of reminds me of a light bulb flicker just before it catches to full light hopefully on the verge of returning to normal, full, and bright." Clearly," I say with emphasis, "Assemblers are already onto me," as I demonstratively lift my foot for all to see, living proof, I think.

"Maybe Assemblers are now aware of Jules as well. We need you, Ming's, we need you, Jimmy, we need each other to figure out this Ripfold thing before the Assemblers close us down and turn out the lights on Jules and me."

Ming's is quiet, and Jimmy is taking it all in, so I break the silence. " The obvious thought for me," I start, "these wispy shadows are the remaining essence of real people. Shadows of people, remnants of what they were, likely past Linkers and Loaders like Jules, me, and Jeeves. At one time real people, the shadow that hit me, tackled me into the Ripfold was real enough. Now only shadows or forms of who they were, the only thing left of them in our world. The Loader captured, vanquished, or eliminated by the Assemblers, now lost or buried in a sealed and closed Ripfold."

To myself I think about the Findlay Crawler desperately clinging to the table in our world, attempting to leave its own world until the closing fold sucked it back inside and now likely gone forever. Ming's then jumps in, "And you are thinking the boomerang pile sitting not twenty feet from us outside is remnants of closed Ripfolds? You can see them but can't pick one up, memories now lost forever, since they never happened, they aren't real?" He speaks, then Jules says, "I wondered when Mae's fold closed if we added another boomerang to the pile?" Jules then adds, "The memory did exist, the virus made Mae forget and we were there to help her remember she had the candy money in her pocket. The memory never got performed, the memory will never get performed, she and the Ripfold are gone forever, it no longer exists," Jules sadly concludes.

Ming's adds, "There's one other thing that strikes me, what you and Julia refer to as the Findlay Crawler. Julia indicated that it was not Jeeves, but both of you observing the Crawler being much older, likely a middle-aged male. However, I think it may not have been Jeeves but Jeeves inside another person, as a Loader. Based on what you have told me today, the shadows, boomerangs, your foot,

Jeeves's photos, it would follow. Jeeves knew the Assemblers found him and the Ripfold was closing.

"Jeeves may have already reconnected with his former self. You were likely tackled by Jeeves's essence.

"Therefore, both were now inside the Ripfold, possibly or even likely inside the Crawler. Jeeves then must use the only way he knew to escape, to try and live our world inside a body from the Ripfold world. Sounds crazy, I know, but I think it's possible," Ming's concludes.

The three of us headed back to Evandale. There's not much to be said, we've said enough already. Then, my phone pings, indicating I have a text. "Check your email, Brandon, I sent you a picture of the Girta crew including Anna, Julia's mom," signed Robert Alcott.

Chapter Ten

"The Linker takes input of object code generated by compiler /assembler /loader and once all the object codes are assembled links, the intended memory action to be accessed or performed."

"Hey, do you think when you go to heaven you get to choose?" Jimmy says. Here we go I am thinking, we have a long drive ahead as the three of us headed to Columbus and Ohio State for spring break and Jimmy is now off and running.

"Okay I am game," I say. "Choose what?"

"Choose what age you want to be, you know say you hit heaven around seventy, you're old, beat up, wrinkly, tired all the time, wondering if you walk up to the Pearly Gates, hey Peter, I am thinking sixteenish or maybe seventeen, seventeen's not bad."

"You're seventeen now," I say. "Seems kind of lame that's the best you can do," I say, egging him on.

"Yeah, kind of liking it though at least right now. Of course, I've got some extracurricular stuff going on," he said, nodding at Jules and me, "most 17-year-olds don't got!"

Jules wants to play along. "I would go for late twenties, which would be cool. I would have this great career, looking good, making big bucks, nice car, and apartment with great view of a downtown somewhere."

"Sounds good, but maybe you can't go for what you haven't been, and you haven't been twenty yet, I am thinking you can only go for what you have already been," I say.

"No way," Jules screams, "that's a dumb rule, this is heaven, in heaven you're supposed to get what you want with instant gratification. Look at this way. If you wouldn't have died you would have gotten there and in my dream, I've gotten to my late twenties presumably heaven and God would know what you were going to be like?" Jules says.

"Yea maybe," I say." I'll give you that, but I think like a game show you only get so many chances," I point out.

"What's that mean," Jules asks.

"Well think about it, how many times they going to let you jump around, just go back and forth? I mean if you're twelve years old one day and want to be thirty next think of all the work. They got to upgrade everything, what you wear, what you eat, where you live, friends, like a yoyo. It would take an army of people working around the clock just to keep up," I finish.

"I don't think anyone's allowed to work in heaven," Jimmy says. "I am thinking probably three times, three times seems about right, things usually come in threes, like underwear and socks," I throw in.

"Where do you buy your underwear these days," Jules asks.

"What underwear?" Jimmy barks back.

After the laughter dies down, Jules jumps back in. "That doesn't work, three doesn't work, it's not fair because what if you pick wrong the last time, the third time. Door number three is a boring job, kids are drug addicts, the wife leaves you for the pool boy. That would be more like hell. Wow maybe that is hell, you must live your life's worst moments, over and over and over. What about the chain thing, remember the chain thing in that movie? The Chain I forged in life? That Christmas show scared the hell out of me as a kid. I got to carry that heavy weight around forever just like that old guy Ebenezer," Jules finishes.

Jimmy now, "I bet when that dude finally got to heaven, the first thing he did was change his name. Everybody in heaven knows him as Ebb."

The three of us go silent for a minute, settling in now. At least another hour to the University.

Ten minutes or so and Jimmy starts back up. "I don't know about you guys, but my mom and dad were over the top about me visiting Ohio State. They probably didn't see me as the college type. My mom sprung for the car and the gas," Jimmy says.

"My Uncle was sound asleep. If I am back before eleven tonight, he won't even notice I was gone," Jules says.

Thinking to myself, Ron and Ally are also both excited I would take my spring break to tour a college even though I am only a junior. Well, next year I will be a junior. My dad's first thought is "I don't know if you will be good enough to play for Ohio State, the best of the Big Ten, but college is about dreaming big," he said at dinner few days ago. He was probably thinking about scholarship money, but I don't really care where I play, I am thinking just want to play basketball that is.

"Remember guys, we are here to drive the campus, visit the Ohio State Institute of Infectious Disease, then Primate Plus," I remind everyone.

"I don't know," Jimmy says." If you ask me, I don't think either of you should go anywhere near that Institute. Better let me handle that one."

"Why would that be?" Jules asks.

"It'll be like the metal detector at the airport or the summer air raid siren back in Sharonville," he says. "You guys will trigger every alarm in the building so loud they will hear it back in Cincinnati."

"Hey, I resemble that remark," says Jules kiddingly.

"Yeah, and who said we are infectious," I throw in.

Jimmy, laughing and shaking his head, says, "you two are really starting to bug me," he follows but also laughs.

"Enough of this," I throw in. "Let's get something to eat, it's already noon and there must be Micky Dees around here somewhere."

We settle in for a few exits. Columbus is about two hours from Cincinnati, so probably another hour in front of us. Jimmy learned to keep the peace with Jules playing Derrick and Dominoes lightly in the background. Jules looking at the picture Mr. Alcott sent. In this picture Anna is front and center, holding a cute baby chimp and surrounded by five or six Girta employees, including Robert Alcott. Each of the employees signed the picture with their name and job title. They were honoring Anna that day, Vendor Day. She is probably in her mid-twenties, beautiful and smiling. One thing that caught my attention. Maria Bunch, Vice President of Human Resources. I make a mental note to visit her when we get back to see if she can help me identify other kids. Kids about my age, our age, Julia, and me, past Girta prodigy.

Jimmy back to wondering out loud the benefit of touring the Institute.

"You know Jimmy, I think you may be right about the Institute," Jules follows. "What are we supposed to do there?" Jules wonders out loud.

"Guys chill out, we got to start somewhere," I respond. "Right now, we got Ming's and Alcott. We need more input, more data, one day we might need the Institute," I finish.

"Yeah, well one day," Jimmy says, "the Institute may need us." All three of us point and yell about the same time. The sign says McDonalds next exit and off we go.

It's now early afternoon. We spent about an hour touring the campus of Ohio State. It's way large for me. A smaller campus is more my style. Jules and Jimmy are mostly silent maybe for similar but different reasons. None of us seem compelled, so we all decide time to move on and head out to the other targets.

Now pulling into the parking lot of the Ohio State Institute of Infectious Disease, we pull in and follow the signs to the main building. There, staring us in the face to the right of the main building past the sidewalk area and berm but before the tree line, the largest Ripfold I have ever seen. I didn't see a single fold in and around the University, now the apparent front door right in front of us. The Ripfold, like a large sliding glass window, partially open not a fold as we know it, more rigid and rectangular nothing natural about it, and probably the equivalent of fifty folds. You could easily walk up, lift a leg, and slide inside as it starts about three feet off the ground. Well, we think it is a Ripfold, Jules is seeing and sensing the same thing. It is compelling. Jules and I both feel it, sense it is drawing and enticing us to come inside same or the similar sense I typically get. Not as powerful, not as strong, but similar. We both try to describe to Jimmy what we see, how we feel he sensed something amuck. He is good about that, but he indicates there is nothing there, at least nothing he can see. Jimmy is willing to walk up to it, he says, and we could guide him via phone, he points out.

Not sure why, but I am thinking we should first reach out to Ming's, see what he thinks, see what he knows. We all agree so call him put the phone on speaker and when he answers, we describe where we are and what we see.

"Wow you guys get around," Ming's says. "I am impressed. What are you guys doing at the Institute?"

"It's a long story," I say to Ming's. "Any idea what this large window might be, the window we just described?"

"Yes, based on what you have said, I believe It's the Compiler," Ming's says without hesitation. "At least it's supposed to function like a Compiler, a modified Compiler and makeshift Ripfold, only the fold is a one-way street for Linkers and Loaders. Don't go near it, and whatever you do don't try to enter it. If I am right, you will not come back," he warns. "I'm not sure how it was re-created in

Columbus. It would be interesting to find out someone very clever and still active in this research area," Ming's says, thinking out loud.

Ming's continues, "My dad and I were originally contracted to work this project in Dayton at Wright Patterson Air Force Base. The contract award didn't really have a name commissioned under a large IDIQ contract meaning indefinite delivery indefinite quantity. IDIQ is a contracting vehicle often used by the Federal Government. IDIQ awards use the trickle-down theory to divvy out specialized contract work; the further down it trickles the harder it is to find, limited visibility, little accountability, and indefinitely intended. I doubt anyone working for the Institute even knows it exists, the Compiler that is, except whomever might be responsible for creating or moving it from Dayton," Ming's indicates.

"Years ago, when the government seized the Girta project assets and took control of the program, my dad and I were persuaded to help with the transition.

"Asylum, deportation, and even jail time are pretty good incentives to encourage cooperation. We were asked, 'asked'," Ming's says again with sarcastic emphasis, "to transition activity related to the Girta viral research program. The people in charge were no longer interested in pursuing the work, no longer interested in exploiting the research. The virus was out of hand, creating more problems than it was worth, real or perceived. They needed a way to attract and contain the virus. A deliverable that would act to end the project and any future repercussions, so my dad and I were paid to create that Compiler.

"In all honesty, we didn't know if it would work, we still don't. You guys will remember the simple formula for formatting computer memory; the Compiler uses source code to generate object code. The Linker then takes the object code and creates executable files. The Loader delivers the executable files to main memory. Pretty simple, memory restored, straight forward process. Our objective was to use a Compiler to attract the virus; the Linkers and Loaders. We used this basic approach in the design," he says.

"Interestingly, you can expose it, physically, I mean," Ming says. "You can make it visible. A simple strobe like light beam directed at the window will make it visible to others. People like Jimmy, myself, and those at the Institute."

As Ming's says this, I recall the light that emanated from the Fold at Findlay Market, the flashing light like a strobe exposing the Crawler.

"Now what," I say out loud to everyone. "Where do we go from here?"

"Sounds like the Compiler is 'Hotel California' for Jules and me."

"My advice," Ming's jumps in, "is to leave it alone for now. Probably minimal data coming from the Assemblers relating to your and Jules's Ripfold activities, as evidenced by your foot reappearing.

"Likely no one is paying much attention, on the other hand, the device appears to be operable and working as you can see it and indicate being drawn to it. This device is linked to the Assemblers; one continuous loop helps put us one step ahead of our pursuers. This might also help us find the Assemblers before they find the two of you, based on Jeeves's history and your foot; reprogramming, controlling, or destroying the Assemblers is probably our highest priority," Ming's concludes.

"I like the way you think," Jules exclaims.

Primates Plus is east of town, about a thirty-minute drive from the Institute. We are zapped of energy, and the ride is quiet and subdued. We'll likely make this a quick visit and head back; the very thought of such a concerted effort to find and destroy us is unnerving. Keeping under the radar seems prudent. Jules, however, will not be easy to hold back or even slow down. She has already made reversing the virus impact on others memory her calling, her service, she and Binky kindred souls.

Primate Plus is in a small aging office warehouse complex off Highway I-71 in a light industrial area outside of Columbus. Mr. Alcott pointed us to the company as the sole remaining supplier of test animals for Girta. The company is on the end cap of an older building, a small office at a hard corner with what we assume is access to the warehouse behind. The web page is simple and refers to the parent company, Primate Plus. Primate Plus is favored by medical companies as it is well known for its humane approach to animal testing often sending the tested animals to Primarily Primates; Primarily Primates is a South Texas based not for profit sanctuary with world -wide reach.

The mission is the care and comfort of abused and abandoned animals, often the recipients of pharmaceutical testing and or unnatural training.

The objective is to bring these animals into the Primarily Primate ecosystem with focus on the care, recovery, and quality of life remaining.

We pull up to the office. No cars are in sight, probably all around in the back. As we walk up the lights are on, the door unlocked. We step in but no one is around.

"Probably in the back," Jimmy says. Why don't you guys hang, and I'll go check it out." Sending Jimmy like sending in the marines I am thinking but off he goes, disappearing into the warehouse. Jules is casually looking at the pictures on the wall as I take a seat. Not a minute later, the door opens off to the left behind a temporary wall a woman comes out sees us and says hello.

"Well, we don't get many visitors here. How may I help you?" she asks. I stand to introduce myself and am just about to start the story line the three of us rehearsed on the drive over when Jules exclaims, "That's my mom, that's her!"

She is face to face, not six inches from a framed picture on the main wall. She pulls out and unfolds the picture from her back pocket and holds it up to confirm. I walk up to her and look over

Jules's shoulder. It's Anna. The woman behind the desk comes around to see what Julia is referring to. She looks at the picture on the wall, looks at Julia, does it again, then a third time for good measure." Well, I'll be, maybe we should all sit down," she says.

Helen is her name, probably in her early fifties, fresh look with youthful energy now sitting at the only desk, Jules and I sitting in the chairs directly across and facing her. She has been with the company for many years, joining the company about the time Jules's mother, Anna, disappeared, she explains.

"I never knew her," Helen says." When I joined the company, relative to your mom, everyone was recovering from her disappearance. Do you know much of what happened?" Helen asks Jules.

"No, nothing, nothing at all. I didn't even know what she looked like until just a few weeks ago," Jules explains.

This comment makes Helen pause. She is either choosing her words or wondering if this is really something Jules should hear from her, a stranger. Then Helen gets up, goes over to the picture on the wall and removes it, brings it back and puts it down in front of Julia.

"Honey," she says, coming around the desk to sit back down, "the man standing to the right of your mom at the time of this picture was general manager of the company. I worked for him, a good man. I enjoyed working with him. Do you recognize or know him?" she asks, looking toward Jules and pointing to the picture.

Julia grabs the frame, I think first looking again at her mom then at the man next to Anna.

"No, ma'am," she says politely.

"Well," Helen says without hesitation, "I am thinking he is your father."

After a bit of time Helen talks about Anna's disappearance. "Your mother was sick and pregnant with you and concerned about three very special chimps. One day soon after you were born, she took you, the chimps, and an old truck and left the building. She was not heard of again until a few years later when a small local hospital in rural northeastern Ohio called. Out of the blue they found evidence she worked here; I took the call, the hospital trying to locate kin, Anna was dying. They were not even sure what was killing her. She had specifically named an aunt and uncle to take care of you, her only child. You were very young at the time. By that time your father, Dan Childs, the man in the picture, was no longer here but working in San Antonio. A few days later, before we could notify Dan, we heard back from the hospital that your mom had passed, next of kin notified and on the way to pick you up. Dan found out soon after that you were gone, he decided it was best for you to have a family and stayed in Texas where he lives today."

"Helen, this might sound like a strange question considering what you just told us, and I know this occurred many years ago, but what happened to the three chimps?" I ask.

She looks at me like I am from outer space, hesitates, then answers, "That is exactly what Mr. Childs asked me many years ago, the very first thing he wanted to know. I feel like there must be more to this story than I understand," she exclaims.

"Welcome to my world," Jimmy says as he walks back in with one of the men from the warehouse. After introductions, Helen settles back in, starts again.

"Once everything was in order after the initial shock from your mother passing, Mr. Childs sent one of our recovery teams up to your mother's compound to inspect, recover, and clean out the area. It's part of what we do. I heard that gravestones of sorts were found for two of the animals with the names Billy and Sean loosely carved into barn wood.

However, one of the grave sites, Sean's, was askew, the bones dug up and remains randomly scattered about.

"Described in the base field notes like a wild animal feast, technicians thought the second chimp was probably recently deceased and buried in a shallow grave. The grave marked Billy was untouched. The third chimp appeared to have been alive and well, living inside the home with Anna, because they found an open cage just inside the main drawing area. A name plate hanging over the cage entrance. KY is the name I remember, as in short for Kentucky. The open cage indicated recent living activity. The team spent a considerable amount of time in the area trying to draw, trap, and capture KY; however, the third chimp was never found."

Helen didn't waste any time letting Dan know the same day about our visit and conversation. That was two weeks ago. Today, she told him about our visit and most importantly about Jules. Her existence is a little awkward for him, so he asked Helen to organize a meeting.

So here we are back to Ming's Chinese Street Food Diner, back to our original table where it all started now just Jules, me, and Mr. Dan Childs. We are meeting Dan for the first time. More importantly Jules may be meeting her dad for the first time. It turns out Mr. Childs may be one of us; well, Billy may be one of us. Billy was probably a Loader, according to Dan, but they referred to it as jumping. Like jumping off a bridge," Billy would say, "into the Little Miami River, Billy, and his friends, up the Foster Bridge and into the river when he was just a boy." It was the first thing Dan asked us when we sat together.

"Do you two see and do things others can't see and do?" he asked without hesitation or pretense. Jules and I both nod yes.

"I figured," was his only response.

"Let's start there," Dan says." I am thinking the two of you do what Billy used to do, what I understand Billy used to do. You have a way to jump time, jump into a warp, as Billy called them. Enter another human to help them, to help them do something they need to do, am I correct?"

Julia and I both look at each other back to Dan, then nod our heads yes.

"Okay thanks, that helps. This gift, I understand, results from a viral strain you were injected with, inherited, or exposed to," he says.

"Yes, sir that's what we believe," I say.

"So, Billy and Anna, maybe Binky," Dan, looking at me as he says this, "probably were also infected." We nodded. "Makes sense," he says. Dan knows he owes Jules an explanation. I can feel him trying to come around to it. Jules looking nervous, probably anxious. I can't blame her.

"Julia, I would start out with how strange this is about to sound, but you already know that. Let me tell you what happened from my perspective, and we can go from there. Your real father is Billy Reynolds. Billy saved my life but gave up on his own. I don't know if that is what he intended. My life was a mess. I won't go into why. Some details are better left unsaid, offing myself, suicide was right there, right in front of me, my immediate future.

"Let me back up. I'm getting ahead of myself. The two of you know how you feel when you jump, you know what it is like to be inside another, correct?"

"Yes," we both say again.

"So, try to be Billy and stand in Billy's shoes knowing what you know as I describe what I felt and what I think happened. Keep in mind I only know what I absorbed from him all these years. II's not like we talk. Billy is still inside me more like my conscience now. Never tried to verbalize this before and it just sounds crazy wild.

"Oh well we are on roll, let's keep going. Billy's last jump into a warp or Ripfold, as you say, was to take this body back with him. This body, my body, the one you see now, Billy was dying, and Anna was pregnant with you," he says as he nods toward Jules. "Anna met Binky through the animal testing service. I think you know that, and at one point the company they worked for terminated the program, with the government seizing all the contract assets. However, they could not seize what was inside of Binky's head. Her experiment was not working, at least not as planned. Binky, your mother Brandon, was also sick. She went inside herself and took to writing." As he says this, he pulls out a few photos and puts them in front of Jules, photos of Anna and a young man another of Anna, the young man, three chimps and Binky.

"For Billy, your father, it all happened rather fast," he continues. "That's him sitting next to Anna. Billy Reynolds was his birth name. Your mother, Julia, was Joanna Trapp. Dan, the person I am now, was about to die, about to commit suicide. Billy was helping me get a few things right before I passed. That's when Billy came up with the idea," Dan says." He and I would leave the warp together, as one.

"You may not know that when you enter a warp or Ripfold, your essence stays behind," Dan says. The essence I now believe is what Jules and I see as wispy clouds or shadows, the shadows or rays circling the Wooster Pike building.

"He did not know; Billy did not know his essence could not join us once we emerged from the warp. Billy and his essence could not reconnect. Dan was not Billy, and Anna could not accept me as Billy. She was right, of course. I was Dan with Billy buried deep inside; her Billy was gone. I believe, Brandon, your mother found a way for a chimp to absorb a person's essence. The chimp took Billy's essence and Anna chose the chimp. Anna found it easier to be with the monkey than with Dan, a person she had never met and didn't know. We kept up the pretense for bit while she was pregnant and then you were born," as Dan looks to Jules. "Families don't get more broken than that. Since you journey into Ripfolds, this tale won't seem so crazy, so strange. Maybe you can understand why soon after you were born your mom disappeared, just picked up and left. I knew why but everyone else was stunned. We both knew the new baby was not mine. She escaped and took to living in the hill country, a single mom with nobody else. She took you and the experimental chimps with her. Not long after, I left for Texas came to San Antonio to work with Primates. Funny at the time I knew very little about monkeys, proof I think that part of Billy was still there, still inside me. We did correspond, Anna and I, from time to time when she needed medicine or information for the chimps. She always used a P.O. Box, however, never went any further than that. Dan is me now, still a little Billy inside. His music Motown, me a country fan, now just happy to be alive. That's the whole story, much more between the lines and a lot of day to day skipped over," he says with a smile. "Part of your father inside of me, another part inside a chimp I'm sorry to say," as he looks at Julia. "No longer with us as the monkey is now dead and buried."

"I almost forgot, Brandon, I found these handwritten notes from your mom. I had them in my possession for some time now, and I thought you might like to have them." He hands me a small, wrinkled paper torn from a notebook with severed edges along the top. Before I look at what he gave me, I ask if he tore it from an actual notebook.

"No," he says." I found this placed inside a novel, like a bookmark about halfway inside one of the classics, Dickens, or Poe, I think, but the title and author escapes me now."

"Binky's note, that note," he says, lightly pointing toward the paper he handed me, "is why I keep these photos, why I always have them with me. I took these and your mother's message from the box of stuff Helen mailed to me, the stuff our crew recovered searching Anna's compound many years ago." While he is saying this he leans over and takes two of the photos, leaving one photo behind, the one with Binky, Anna, Billy, and the chimps.

"You keep that one Julia," he says." These other two I need to help keep me grounded," he adds." Of course, my situation is rather unique, I guess except for the other two chimps," Dan says as he finishes.

Binky knew I was probably one of us, just like Jules and me. Her box in the attic, *The Monkey's Paw*, one of the novels still in the box. Recalling now what Robert Alcott told me as we were leaving the restaurant many weeks ago: "Whatever you are experiencing, I feel certain Binky knew."

The Monkey's Paw is a story about bringing someone back from the dead. Be careful what you wish for I think the underlying theme of the novel, what I remember from my ninth grade reading of *The Monkey's Paw*. Before Dan leaves, I ask if he still has Anna's box where the pictures and books are kept.

"Yes, pushed away somewhere but you are welcome to it," he says.

I indicated to him we will circle back in a few weeks about the box, then we say are thank you and goodbye, Jules walking him outside as I am still seated at the diner.

I pick up and read Binky's note:

"Believe God knows about these wrinkles or folds in the sky, these holes in time choosing to let them exist like Cain and Abel, letting them play out. Separating oneself and jumping into time might be extraordinary, but it's a long way from natural. One thing I have learned upon death, any death, the essence, the deceased essence still exists. It's there, it hangs around. Loved ones can see and feel it, it's real and painful for many. The person, the human is gone is but the essence, like walking into an empty bedroom still full of who they were. To a scientist, the essence really looks like clutter, eventually boxed, binned, gifted, trashed, and sold or stored. Sooner or later memory takes over, pictures remain, the clutter disappears. The person you knew and loved fades now, buried for a second time. Believe now the universe looks for and requires balance, Einstein's Theory of Relativity is relevant. The virus clearly infected equilibrium like Brandon's backyard teeter totter, now one end stuck soundly upward pointing to the sky, needing balance."

Early evening the next day Jules and I are walking to meet Jimmy then down to the Wooster Pike warehouse. This morning, I grabbed *The Monkey's Paw* from the box in the attic. I now have it with me, rolled up in my back pocket like a newspaper to give to Ming's. I feel certain Binky is buried deep inside and behind the print. The conversation with Dan has taken its toll and I unload this to Jules as we walk. She thinks I am too practical, too logical, think too much. All we know, she says, is that someone needs us. In her mind it doesn't really matter what else is at stake. I am more confused, wondering out loud to Jules if this strange journey we are on is worth it. We have learned a lot recently, and now know we are way out on a ledge, a dangerous ledge. Flip side, if I stay, focused coach thinks I will play college basketball. Who knows, maybe NBA or Europe in my future, I say to Jules. Most importantly a full ride and basketball might pay my way to college. Jules does not respond; she is listening. We could have a normal college life, I say, no Ripfolds, no Assemblers, no dark shadows, you know, a normal life.

This all sounds pretty good, but it might also mean no Jules, Jimmy, or Ming's, no team, I think to myself but don't say this out loud. Jules just stares at me giving me that "look" she has like I have no clue, not quite an idiot but clearly no clue. Finally, she says, "It may be for just a flash, only a flash or brief moment, this may be all life or death gives a person, but if its strong enough, compelling enough then Maude, Olaf, and Claude happen, Mae could have happened," she says, "We happen.

"I don't know or care why a Ripfold forms from this, when it does, or how it does, that's us, that's me, that's you, that's what you and I do, what could be better than that," she says, smiling.

I think to myself this may be Binky in disguise, ten years later. Already walking next to the only thing, I know, is more exciting than basketball. Looking at Jules then myself, I realize, with a smile all body parts present and accounted for, that's a good start. Binky put me on this path, she did this for a reason. There must be a big picture here somewhere. I probably need to see it through. As I am thinking this, Jimmy "the Greek" pulls up alongside the two of us. I knew it was him approaching, Metallica could be heard blocks away. Now passenger side window down, radio down but not off, "hey dynamic duo," he screams, "ready to change the world?"

PRELUDE TO PART II

Brandon, Jules, Jimmy, and a perceptive young scientist named Ming's have come together only to discover they are very different. Their world is very different. Their future is shaped by the dark shadows and torn remnants of a virus. The virus's sole focus is to steal a person most vulnerable memory before it occurs. The contagion freely and with targeted abandon changing lives and pilfering the free will of the infected.

The teens' mission: to restore the memories the virus is currently trying to steal before the theft occurs and eradicate or neutralize the virus forever. The four team members; Brandon, Jules, Jimmy and Ming's, also know there were others that came before them that knew and entered the Ripfold. More importantly they know there are others like them alive today. At least one little girl in Texas with the same gift to jump into the Ripfold. Presumably with the same mission of restoring the infected's original desire and memory. For those like them that have gone before, only remnants remain. The Ripfold extracts a price. Each time one of the carriers enters a fold, their spirit or essence stays behind in this world while the Folder or person enters the body of another in their world. In their time and space to repair that person's memory. If the Folder does not return, the essence lives alone wandering forever like hungry rays or shadows. The original Folder existing only as a divided shadow and human inside another. The lost souls only hope, the hope of those split by the Ripfold, that our young foursome will find a way to bridge and forge their lives together again. Out of the Ripfold world and back to their own, reunited.

The team recently became aware of a few, just a few infected, alive today and living in Texas; Katherine, who worked for Girta and her young daughter Cat. Cat is young, inexperienced, and vulnerable. A common Ripfold journey between Brandon and the young girl is the only form of communication. Our teens know; however, the clock is ticking. Something needs to happen soon.

As always it seems there is a lot going on in the Lone Star State.

PART II
SOMETHING WICKED

Chapter One

Jules knew she had to know; she went first, what a set up. Here I am bouncing along about three feet from the ground, nose up, trotting along, really all four legs in motion. All four feet pounding forward. I feel hungry but think I am always hungry. Lucky she is not within sniffing distance, Jules, that is. Her left leg would be toast, soaked by now. She and Jimmy are probably having a field day over this Ripfold journey. I can hear them laughing. Oh, wait got a sniff, got a smell large rock and pole, off we go, likely that Great Dane down the way. Curtis is thinking, the one with all the fur. Check it out, yep, that's her, lift my leg, leave a bit behind and off we go. I can pee at will, one of my many talents, me and Curtis, Curtis the dog.

Curtis is a large white dog with black spots, a few black spots along the torso looks like my head is mostly brown, the ears black, face like a retriever. We can see our reflection in the neighbors' windows as we trot past, making our morning rounds. We have now passed three vehicles with Texas plates, one labeled temporary TX April 21, 2017, all right at eye level, hard to miss but me with a front row seat, how cool is that I am in Texas.

The only surprise in Anna's belongings, the package Dan sent to Jules this week containing Anna's box of stuff; a few torn pages or ripped fragments of letters between Dan and Anna, a handful of books, classic novels really, a picture or two and a Ripfold. Yes, a Ripfold. I doubt he knew it but went along for the ride. This is how I know Jules is enjoying my doggy daycare romp. As is typical, she jumped first.

Life as a dog, large dog, probably go 110 lb., bad ass to some, friendly to most. Only five minutes, but I'm already getting used to it. I am wearing a collar but have not seen a reflected tag. Another smell and off we go again.

Thoughts or communication between myself and Curtis is delayed, like watching a basketball game on two screens, one clearly a split second in front of the other. Not sure why or where we are headed, lots of distractions all around us, at this rate our journey together could take a while. I take that back, off we go, seemingly this time with purpose. Off to the left more of a hurried pace down a short hill. Now along a worn trail leading to a large creek bed, dry creek bed, bone dry creek bed, clearly the junction point for two flood plains coming together. Receded for now, a perfectly silent roaring white-water intersection. Washed rock and crevices everywhere large and small, scrub trees and sage all around guessing lizards, snakes, scorpions, and other varmints are patiently waiting out the sun. It's late morning and the sun is high but not hot, not for Texas. We are cruising along the riverbed to the starboard side when suddenly Curtis stops, pivots left, jumps down into hole, a rock outcropping probably three feet of drop. It's deep enough to feel brief coolness as we hit bottom shelf like rock. He knows what he is doing and where we are, he has been here before. I can sense this.

Now I see it, see something off to the right, kind of looks like a person, a girl, a young woman I believe. She is stuffed or rolled into the rock shelf covered in dead leaves and detritus, blood and not much else. One dangling tennis shoe that I can see. Curtis goes right up to her as we are now sniffing. I believe she is still alive, but I can't see or sense anything moving, nothing at all. My mind is blazing, crazed, holy shit, holy shit I keep screaming to only myself. Instinctively, I reach out to touch her, to feel for a pulse. Damn, that got nowhere like being in a sealed glass box. Curtis is now taking over as he is down on his haunches next to her, licking the wounds and gashes to her lower abdomen just above her navel, multiple wounds. I am trapped, seeing only through Curtis, his eyes doing only what Curtis can do. Now watching what he has been doing, he is licking, he has been licking, and it is working. At least there is no blood coming from her, just around her. Her face appears beaten badly, her head awkwardly twisted toward the inside of outcropping, her legs are also mangled. I can't really see much else, seeing her face is not a priority for Curtis.

Get it together, Brandon, I say to myself. You are here for a reason, why are you here, I am screaming to myself, think, think what Curtis can do. As my mind starts to come around, I start to focus. He is licking, that is good, but I don't think he knows what to do next, what else, what else can a dog do, I think to myself. What can he do that I cannot. He can smell, I say loudly to only me, He can smell. She was likely dragged here and rolled up inside to rot. She left a trail. We can find and follow a trail. He can follow a scent, so we need that sneaker, we need to focus on the sneaker. There is no other clothing remnant in site, nothing that I can see. My urge is to grab him by his ears, shake his head, and force him toward the sneaker. Instead, I have another idea. Dogs do a couple of things better than us, one of them much better than me. I take my right hand, place my index finger and thumb partly inside my mouth, roll back my tongue a bit and create a small space between my lips and fingers, then blow. A whistle my dad taught me many years ago. Curtis's ears go up immediately. He jumps to all fours. Dogs can hear, Curtis can hear. I am staring at the shoe. I can't do much else. I keep staring, but he looks away. I whistle again, now he is back at attention. Like the morning roll call at West Point, Curtis is now marching forward toward the shoe. He is getting it, our thinking is starting to synch. This is one smart dog. He loosens the strings with his mouth, lightly tugs at the front part of the shoe. We have it in our mouth then when he pulls off the shoe, I hear it, low, very low less than a stifle more than a breath. My heart pounds, my inside explodes. Did I just hear that or was it bird, branch, or wind? Again, lighter now, there it is again. The dog hears it too, his head down still holding the shoe in his mouth. Curtis turns toward the girl but when he does, the shoe drops to the ground. Bottoms up, crap, we then take one step forward toward her, toward the girl. When we take the step our right front paw, leg, and weight inadvertently settle on the shoe, pushing it deep into the surrounding grime, sludge, blood, and dirt.

Sometimes it's good to be lucky rather than right. This is one of those times. The top of the shoe is pushed into the ground, shoestrings soaking it up like a straw. The blood; a dark red, dirty maroon, now my favorite color. We need to focus, so fingers now back to my mouth, we need to keep moving. Only God knows how long we have. I blow hard to whistle again. Curtis, immediately at full attention, starts to back up. Move on and move out, but I blow hard again. He hesitates, appears to understand, moves forward, and clamps the rubber bottom of the shoe in his powerful jaws. We are off and quickly out of the crevice, two long easy jumps. I wish I had these legs on the court, I am thinking. Not much of a leaper myself, off we go with four-legged abandon. At first, we followed the same line we did in-coming. Then, without warning, we deviate to the left up the ravine and out of the gulch. Now climbing in brush, thicket, and steep slope very narrow path, every plant in Texas meant to poke, cut, stick, or slice. I don't know where we are headed, but I like our chances. He knows what he is doing, following a scent is my guess. We stop a little past halfway. Curtis, head down, smells something strong with the shoe still in tow. We are sniffing around large, exposed oak roots, stretched to breaking, but not yet ready to give way. The trees resolve a testament to the clash and force of the raging creek. We are twenty feet above the ravine. There it is wedged between two large roots, a small brown grocery bag, barely visible, partially torn, spilling clothing and other personals.

I whistle again. I don't want to get too distracted. I don't think the bag is going anywhere. Off we go again without warning. In minutes we are at the side yard of where we started, his house, his home. Now around to the back and through the double netted door opening to the TV room as we burst through the magnets settle the two sides of the loose net back together again, closing behind us. Now the part I am dreading, as this will not be easy, I am thinking.

"Hey big guy where you been?" I hear coming from the man in the lounge chair facing the TV monitor. "Did you take off running again," he says, addressing Curtis and now turning to look at us. Curtis slowly approaches him, shoe still in tac. "What you got there?" he asks. "Another one of mom's tennis shoes?" Then, "what the heck," I hear him say as he gets a closer look. Curtis is now almost within reaching distance. The man's arm lunges out to grab the shoe and Curtis pulls his head and the shoe back to the right, just in time, just out of his reach. Now the man is at attention, no whistle needed he wouldn't hear it anyway, as he stands up and starts to come towards us.

"What you got there boy?" he says as he kneels next to the dog I whistle once again and hopefully for the last time. Curtis hears it and moves away, walking quickly down long straight hallway. I see where he is going, the front door. We walk up and stand, our nose inches from the door waiting, the man following just behind and now down on one knee next to the dog.

"What on God's green earth…" his voice trails as he now has the shoestring gently looping the fingers of his right hand. "This does not look good, pray it's not what I think it is," he says out loud. The man stands up, quickly moves toward the table in an adjoining room, leans over, picks up a leash, a set of keys, and his cell phone. Back to Curtis, leash attacked, and front door cracked open, cell phone slipped into his back pocket. Curtis squeezes out, pushes the door wide, leaps proudly onto the porch and Bang, I am gone.

I slam hard into the back outside wall of the diner, exiting the Ripfold. My essence and I are long overdue for a talk, but I am stunned either way. I walk over to patio table around the back of Ming's and flop down in Ming's Chinese Street Food diner. I don't ever remember sitting outside, probably too cold before. I didn't even notice they had a patio. My mind, not even sure where to start, clearly on overload, but I am glad to be back on my own two feet. I think I will just sit here for a while, why not, nothing better to do. It feels good just to bring my hands together and watch my arms bend;

fold and unfold my hands a couple of times, stand up then sit back down, stand up then sit back down. Just for grins, I flex my hands, arms, and feet feels good to be back I am thinking, wanting to say back to normal but don't think my life qualifies anymore.

As I sit there, I realize I don't really know anything about the girl, the young woman in the rocks. I know or believe she was in Texas, now thinking San Antonio since Dan is there. This would account for the appearance of the virus. Thinking the dog caught the virus licking the girl's wounds, the girl was my likely target, Jules will know. My newly acquired canine instincts, I think kiddingly, tell me viruses, like Texans, don't like boundaries or fences. I do remember that one of the license plates carried a date, it was one of those paper dealers' plates that normally signify a new car. The new plate was dated April 21, 2017. It's time to reach out to Jules, I am thinking, to learn what she knows, but I just don't have the energy right now. Back to sitting for a while, vegging out seems like a good idea. Sitting here seems like a good idea might play rock, paper, scissors with myself, just to play with my fingers and hands, see who wins. I laugh.

I think I nodded off as the sun starts to set and it gets colder fast. I'm now awake and texting Jules to see if she wants to meet at Ming's.

"Been sitting here for over an hour waiting for you-worried," was her immediate response. Now I feel like the big dog just sitting here all that time. I go quickly around to the front and inside the restaurant. Just as the sun sets for good behind the building, she sees me come in and quickly stands up next to the booth. I walked right up to her with a smile put my arms around her, and bear hug her. I pick her straight up to face height, plant a big kiss, then set her back down and just stand holding her for a while. She seems fine with this, her slight frame blending, disappearing into mine instantly.

Diane, the waitress, comes up behind us. We hear, "You kids going to just stand there all night?" Both look behind us, laugh, and scamper clumsily into the back side of the booth. "About time you two got together," Diane says with a warm motherly smile. Pen and paper in hand now, she is poised and ready to take our order. I'm not sure why, she won't need it. Both Jules and I turn to look up at her and without hesitation, "the usual," we say in sync.

"Two chicken ramen and Cokes?" she confirms.

"Yes please," our response and off she goes.

Jules, with no hesitation, digs right into her Ripfold visit. The girl's name was Katherine. She was thirty-one. She was at a common local eatery but sitting at the bar. Jules believes somewhere in San Antonio because the Spurs, the local basketball team, was on every television screen, including the largest one over the center area.

"I know this only because they kept screaming, Go Spurs Go, every few minutes, a large, raucous, fun crowd surrounding us," she says. The month of April often determines the NBA playoff picture, I think to myself. Jules was aware enough of the surrounding circumstance to mindfully record an older gentleman watching game to the left and a younger, larger man near Katherine's age to the right. The younger man and Katherine had hit it off and each seemed to have some vague recognition of the other, neither of them paying attention to the game.

"My visit was short," Jules says. "When I jumped to Katherine, the man almost immediately off to the bathroom, indicating he would be right back. The bartender asked about drink refills. Katherine declined for both. She is training for a marathon run in four weeks.

"My only memory," Jules says, "a business card had dropped to the floor, and I prompted Katherine to pick it up and put in her jean back left pocket. That was really it. I was gone soon after and even before he returned."

Wow, I am thinking to myself, if these two Ripfold experiences are connected, they are worlds apart. I start slowly; this will not be easy to recant. It was hard enough to be there from inside Curtis, much less try to describe to Jules what happened. I have no way of knowing if Katherine was the girl in the rocks, I say, but my gut tells me she was.

She had been beaten badly and left for dead; however, she was alive kind of, a dog, a very smart dog found her. Curtis was his name. Katherine was well hidden, stuffed inside a rock overlook, more of a crevice or hole, the overlook inside a wide now dry, double creek bed. Not visible or discoverable except perhaps by a dog, there was a bag full of clothes hidden or thrown somewhat nearby. Again, only a dog could have found them. I'm guessing the bad guy assumed a solid rain or two would wash away the evidence of either or both. Help was on the way when I was thrown out of the Ripfold, I do not know the outcome or the result. I want to believe she was rescued and recovering. At least physically, If the young man was the culprit, I hope they nail him, God can fill in the blanks.

Jules listens then asks, "Where were you, who were you helping?"

"Great question," my response. "I was Curtis the dog, but believe I was supposed to be inside Katherine. Weird twist of fate that I ended up inside her canine rescuer. Curtis was licking the woman's wounds, and my guess took in some of the virus."

Diane arrives with dinner, and we settle in a bit. Being inside an animal seriously freaked me out, I tell Jules, but somehow, we figured it out. Curtis and I made it work; I think we made a good team, but truth be told, I tell her would prefer not to be a dog again any time soon.

Jules looks at me for a bit then says, "What do think about a large mature female chimp actually, a large mature female bonobo. Chimps and bonobos are often confused," Jules quickly adds.

Kiddingly, I instantly respond, "They got arms and legs, can't be all that bad."

She hesitates before responding. We both ladle a few spoons of ramen in between, now we are both looking at each other.

"You going to tell me why?" I ask.

"Well," Jules starts, "while you were in Texas, Robert Alcott sent us both an email. Clearly you haven't seen it yet. Remember when Helen at Primates Plus was giving us the background on my mom's compound?" Jules adds,

"Sure," I respond.

"She indicated that KY the chimp was never discovered, KY the bonobo was never found," she continues.

"Okay yep, remember that well," I say. "She wasn't found because Alcott found her first. KY has been in the Cincinnati Zoo all these years; KY is there now."

"One other thing you need to know, Brandon," Jules says." Look at me," she requests, now looking me right in the eye, waiting for me to return the gaze. Once we are focused together, she continues, "Alcott believes that KY…is short for Binky."

Chapter Two

The Monkey's Paw is not really a novel but more of a short story, a few cryptic chapters. Sometimes less is more, the Bible in a word, Hemingway a sentence, WW Jacobs a few sparse chapters. The paw exists as Jacobs states, an "ordinary little paw dried to a mummy," said to grant the holder three wishes. It is, however, impossible to wish without consequence. This of course is not apparent to the current owner clouded by its power. As I am thinking this, I remember Ms. Spragen's rule to we kindergarteners, "for every action there is an equal and opposite reaction." Binky knew or figured this out. I don't even have to look beyond the intended prose of WW Jacobs's story. I know what lurks there with the paw, what Ming's will unfold. My favorite author as a kid was Ray Bradbury, the title of my favorite book, *Something Wicked this Way Comes.*

It's Saturday morning, the first day of May and it's raining hard, and I am still waking up. Earlier Jules texted me, much earlier, "the Ripfold with Anna's box is still here," she types." We did not fulfill the memory."

"What!" I reply, about an hour later, "Good morning Mr. Sunshine about time you woke up, you big slug," her only response.

A few hours later that same day, mid-afternoon, the rain slows and then stops. My stepmom Agnes is happy to drop me off at Julia's house. They like her, me too. Upstairs in her room now, I didn't get to see her this week, didn't like that much. Her Uncle downstairs out cold, snoring while watching an NBA game. Napping through the first half, gaining energy for the second, the national pastime. In Jules room with Katherine's Ripfold, it's my turn to jump right in, wanting and hoping this time I land with my own two feet, not all four. I reach and touch the Ripfold and Bang I am gone.

Her name is Katy, but she is known as Cat and we are whipping along on her bike, it's a whirlwind. Big fat tires with bright purple trim handlebars faced down cruising style with micro shift gears a part of the hand brakes. I'm guessing she is thirteen or so as we cruise town, just Cat and me. Riding together, we are taking in the day, and it feels good. I'm not sure what the Ripfold mission is yet, but I see no reason to hurry, this is too much fun. Wait, I think to myself, Cat, Katherine…am I back in Texas? She whips her head around at the first parked car we pass. Sure enough, Lone Star plates, Texas flag embedded in each to remind those who forget. Cat, I am guessing, is likely Katherine's daughter, but I can't confirm this now. I don't know where we are headed, but she does. Little girls always seem on a mission, boys, not so much. Not five minutes later we quickly turned up a drive to the left. She instinctively pops a small wheelie as we jump the curb. Into the open garage, no cars, slight brake only as we wheel hard to the right and skid to a stop. The bike now facing the house, side door, our ride secured and now like a flash we are inside the short hallway. That didn't take long through the kitchen and headed up the back stairs to our room. We need to get something that we forgot last time.

Half-way up, right before the sharp left turn to the next stair level, I stop, we both stop. Now, looking to the right, two mysteries are solved in a single glance. Hanging on the wall in the bevy at the turn along with numerous other pictures, awards and memorabilia is a plaque: Congratulations Katherine Heard, Salesperson of the Year, Girta Technologies 1999. Signed TJ Singh, CEO and Robert S. Alcott, President. There's a picture of all three standing center stage with a large Girta sign dominating the landscape behind them. Katherine worked with my mom, I am thinking, well at least she worked at Girta. Cat, her daughter, moves fast, so did her mom. Within seconds, we are up the remaining stairs into her room. We grab a small picture, and we are off again.

******

Standing in line for tickets with Jules, it's a beautiful sunny day, early May, chilled but warming. We step up to a window counter and ask for two adult tickets although technically Jules qualifies as a child, and I promptly remind her of this. Of course, you know, I say as I handed her the ticket, this means you are in my custody and control, me being the only mature adult present. She promptly retaliates with a smack to the arm.

"Hey, that reminds me," I say as I stare at my arm, "this is like our second date."

What," she exclaims out loud, "what would you call the fifteen times we met at the diner, or Mainliner-you douche-bag," smacking me again harder, the other arm this time. Good to see our form of communication hasn't changed, except for the bruising.

We are together at the Cincinnati Zoo and Botanical Garden. It's late morning and we have all day. We're heading over to the primate area but not in any hurry. Jules wants to start our zoo journey together counterclockwise.

Counter to the crowd and tour, works for me. Just walking in the European style gates makes you relax a bit. Not sure how they do that, maybe the shaded, wide walkways not much yet to command attention, that helps. Like the average visitor, the exhibits aren't going anywhere. They will still be there when we round the bend.

Jules has something on her mind, I can feel it but figure she will get to it soon enough. We are walking up a low-grade hill towards Africa. This might take a while.

"Did you ever Google about Katherine, see what happened?" Jules asks.

"No," I reply. "I didn't really want to know. I worried she was maybe too far gone. Deep down just want to believe she lived and recovered or is recovering. I pray about it at night when I am alone."

We walked silent for a while, her memory of Katherine being very different from mine. Jules points out the little animal prints embedded in the sidewalk as we move forward. Our printed guide indicating these predict the next exhibit, nature's own signage, I think to myself.

"Something I saw when I was inside Katherine at the restaurant," Jules says. "I haven't had a chance to tell you I saw another Ripfold when I was inside Katherine. We saw another fold I should say. It registered with her but she had no internal response that I could feel. The Ripfold was in the main dining area of the restaurant. it was up against the far-left wall near a server station, next to a large painting. It looked normal, the Ripfold, that is, like the ones we see. Nothing out of the ordinary about it that I could tell except one thing," she indicates. "I wasn't drawn to it, wasn't attracted to it, in any way, I could see it, but I wasn't compelled to reach for it," she finishes.

I'm not sure what to say to that, and don't really want to dig too deep, so back into Katherine.

We eventually find our way to Africa and the monkeys labeled Gorilla World here at CZBG. We don't know which one might be Binky, assuming there is a Binky. We haven't asked around or let anyone know we were coming, just acting on Mr. Alcott's email to us. We were thinking this would be fun way to get out together, spend a day.

Binky seems as good a name as any for a full-grown, female bonobo. At CZBG the true apes, various chimps and bonobos are in separate compounds.

Reading the unilluminated marker in front of the exhibit, Bonobos, like chimpanzees, are considered great apes, endangered and believed to be limited to the Congo area of Central Africa. Usually, they are no bigger than two and half to three feet tall and can live upwards of forty years. Like me, they have longer arms than legs to help them navigate trees. For me, it's basketball players. It says here that the bonobo is mankind's closest living relative with 98 percent of our DNA in common. Like us, they often stand upright, have families and even part their hair down the middle. My hair is too thick to part, and Jules wears her brunette locks like a crown on top of her head kind of like the capuchin monkeys next door, both cute as can be.

Probably best to keep this thought to myself. My upper arms will thank me later. There are a few chimpanzees and assume bonobos in this large indoor-outdoor exhibit from young to old. Unless Binky is separated out for whatever reason, there is no way to know which one she might be. Almost as soon as I say this, however, I see it. I was not expecting this. Up near a felled tree structure along a hillside with a chimp or bonobo there is a Ripfold, like a neon sign for Jules and me, judging now by the hair a bonobo. This great ape is comfortably laying on a bed of spruce limbs and pine needles. I'm noticing now for the first time there are numerous spruces, white pine, and bamboo throughout the exhibit. I use my left index finger and arm to point to it meaning the Ripfold and what Alcott believes is Binky.

Jules looks in the right direction but doesn't see it. She verbally remarks to me the bonobo lying on the spruce bed, no Ripfold to her in sight. Try again to confirm, nothing.

"Well, that's different," I say out loud to Jules.

I don't think this has come up before now I wonder if there are Ripfolds, she sees that I can't and vice versa like Katherine maybe.

In any event we know our target we are not going up there, Binky, the bonobo not coming down here. So, I grab my phone and take a picture. This probably ought to play with my mind, I am thinking, but I don't really feel that.

Seeing bonobo in this habitat, these surroundings, if Binky is inside of it, I'm not sure we will ever know. It doesn't stir anything inside of me, well once again maybe I spoke too soon. Phone back in my pocket, I turn to look at Jules. Now she's doing the pointing but looking at me. Pointing at KY, I turn to follow her gaze and direction. The bonobo is now on its feet, looking directly down on Jules and me.

The Ripfold also stirs a bit as if attached moving in unison. It's a little freaky, looks weird. The bonobo, standing erect, long arms dangling at her side hands curled upward and dragging ground her head cocking slowly back and forth, right to left, our eyes lock. She's looking directly at both of us. After what seems like a lifetime KY or Binky the bonobo plops back down, butt first grabs from a pile of leaves and starts to feed. She appears oblivious now, no longer interested in the homo sapiens down the way.

******

We are outside the house again back in Texas, Cat and me back on our bike not having gone not ten feet. I left my school picture on the kitchen table. She can't miss it, mom wanted one. Cat is thinking it will help her train for another marathon race. I start to head out when we stop the bike in our own driveway. Both feet are quickly down, and the bike is balanced between our legs. Cat now realizing when we first arrived the garage door was open, mom not home, no car in sight. The door was unlocked, the garage door up and mom not home, this strikes her as odd. She pulls her phone from her back pocket and hits speed dial, but no answer. She then sends a text to Katherine, her mom, hits send. I'm wondering to myself if Katherine is nearby in the creek bed but almost as soon as I think this, Cat steps off bike, lays it to the driveway, walks over to side wall, flips up the electronic pad, and dials in a code. The garage door slowly closes, inching toward the ground now, all good, safe, and secure. Back to the bike, down the drive and off we go. There is an old truck some distance in front of us to the right that appears to be parked, it's on the outbound side, our side. This catches my attention. It was not there before. The vehicle has an Ohio plate, observing license plates apparently is now my new favorite pastime. No matter, we are gaining speed and will soon blow past it.

Without warning, as we approach in less than an instant, the driver's side door is thrown open and wham, we slam right into and immediately crumble. Cat hits her head on the inside of the driver window and is out cold. I am stunned but still somewhat aware inside Cat. We are in a heap between the door and truck. A large man steps out, violently grabs Cat, and like a rag doll tosses us to the passenger end of the vehicle. We slam hard against the far window and door. Upon impact, Cat's phone falls out, sliding into the side door pocket. We hit the bench seat then roll to the foot area under the dash. Vaguely aware that the man has now tossed the bike to the back bed, he's now back in the truck, door closed and shifting down for drive. Only seconds have passed and off we go, this trip now very different from how it started.

"It's the children," he is shouting with great force and anger, "the devil's own, the devil's own," he rants louder and louder. "It is the children," pure wild eyed, mangy hate. The man looks down at us as he is screaming. Now he's attempting to kick us with his right leg while he drives. Both arms now also stretched from the wheel and body maneuvered for leg to reach our back side, misses each time so far, but not for lack of trying. Back and forth from gas to attack mode, truck gyrating, speeding up, slowing down, like a bronco rodeo ride. Finally, the truck swerves deep right and runs aground, he or "It" quickly back in driver's seat, both hands on the wheel now backing up and navigating to roadway. "The devil's own," he keeps saying over and over in a low guttural growl the evil loud and clear. "That whore Katherine," he says, "the evil whore, not her but them, parents doing the devil's work, the seed, the children, the seed." He now has in his right hand a computer printout that was laying on the seat next to him. Kat's right eye is cracked as he starts to wave this back and forth, preaching Pulpit style.

"I will find them; I will find each and every one of the filthy animals," he yells, his voice in Sunday morning preacher mode. "Not of this earth, none of them, not of this earth, infected slime, every one of them," he goes on and on. Cat is on overload, not able to hear or think, nothing but pure fear as she is balled up and wound tight and smack up against the floorboard. Cat's right eye is barely open but is the first thing visible to me other than the flagging computer print-out. Directly above us is an embedded steel plate just below the glove compartment, I read it quickly, Cat not capable.

Scanning the print rather than reading, it's a registration, license of sorts; Primate Plus, Columbus address, long serial number, date, and great State of Ohio seal. Now I recall the Ohio plates just before impact with the car door.

He or "it" now throws the computer print-out directly at us, in a rage, clear and utter frustration. He means it to hit us, but it floats and falls short, and the paper catches halfway on seat and floor. This hides our face from the driver's scowl, and I gaze at Cat's eyes now slowly, carefully opening and closing. I can make out part of the document—a title at the top of the paper; Girta Technol…appears to be a list of names, possibly employees. I want this print-out, I am thinking to myself.

"We want this print-out," I say out loud inside Cat.

We start to get feeling back, we are laying on things, lumpy hard things, we can feel them underneath us. We can also now feel the head pain from slamming into the car door, her arm and entire left side throbbing. The truck rolls on, we are tight enough into the cubby that the ride is not throwing us around much. Cat begins to squirm, trying to reposition slightly without alerting the driver as he seems to be settling in. The truck is just rumbling along the roadway like a loudspeaker in our left ear. I try to get Cat to lift her head a bit. I want to see more. Her phone is in the door pocket and there is a low-grade glow. I am afraid the madman might see it.

At some point I am saying out loud inside of Cat it is more painful to stay hidden than it is to take charge. Time for action, she begins to move now, cooperating, and settles her head a bit higher on the inner wall. I can see better now, the light is not her phone. It's a Ripfold. I can see it; she can see it. I see it through her it's not mine. I don't know why or how I know this, but it's not my Ripfold. It's hers. Cat does not know what it is. I can sense this. She is only thirteen and it scares her, understandably. It is new to her, but she is one of us. She is a Ripfolder. I can't make her grab the Ripfold, I know this. I cannot make her do anything past the memory change. Only she can make that happen. For now, we must lay here vibrating, bouncing, and waiting.

The madman drives in waves, hits the brakes hard, pounds the pedal to take off again and we roll with each wave. Next time he hits the gas our weight will shift forward; we can almost reach the side pocket. At least without drawing attention to ourselves. At that point all Cat needs to do is grab for her phone. She will come close enough to the Ripfold when she does.

The phone is in the door pocket. I say this out loud to myself, repeating this numerous times inside Cat's head, driving home the message to her. She starts to shift her weight with the natural rolling caused by the truck, learning to use the motion, but it's not easy. Each time we do we roll back and forth over the lumps we are laying on, feeling like numerous pairs of hard shoes but no way to know. So far, the driver appears oblivious to our shifting as we are blending with the natural rhythm of the vehicle. More importantly, we need to time this right. Grabbing the phone without the Ripfold jump won't get us very far. The madman will only seize the device and his wrath to Cat will likely be swift and brutal.

The truck is slowing down. He is braking, pumping, braking and we gyrate with the action. The truck abruptly jars to a stop, a sign or light, I am guessing. When the light changes it may be our chance. Sure enough, his lead foot in action, we fire off. We, Cat, and I roll way forward, much further than I expected. She can see her phone. She instinctively reaches for it with her left hand so the driver can't see her movement. Great idea, no help from me. The movement of the truck throws her left hand right to the Ripfold, but just before she pierced it, our right hand reaches up and grabs the computer print-out. For a split-second Cat and I are eye to eye with the Madman. I see him, he now sees us. Something very familiar in that face flashes across my mind. He now knows we are up to something and reaches toward us with his right hand. His large body weight shifting for leverage, his left hand on the wheel. Cat's hand is about to pierce the Ripfold. His arm is like an arrow aiming for our neck. He hits the brake, bright flash, and Bang we are gone, the truck slamming into a light pole, dead stop.

I am thinking or maybe I am just confused. Is it possible, even likely, that I am in Cat. Cat's Are the journeys overlapping, crisscrossing, colliding? As I start to ponder this, a more pressing thought starts to grow inside me. If this is correct, once Cat's fulfills her memory she may be thrown out in or near the truck and back to where we started. Thrown back into harm's way. Possibly right back to the truck floorboard, at least that's what I assume could happen. That's what sometimes happens to me.

We are back in the kitchen at Cat's house. Katherine picks up the small neatly trimmed sixth-grade photo of Cat. "Wow, my little baby is getting so big looking like a little lady now," Katherine says out loud. "Lots of her dad in her." She can see this in and around her eyes. She turns it over. "Hi Mom Guess, Who," Cat has written in bright red on the picture. She remembered, Katherine is thinking to herself as she walks out onto the front porch and turns to lock the door. Time to stretch, Cat's earlier text indicated soccer practice this afternoon but back for dinner, couple of hours for a run and now what to do with this photo, she is thinking. She has new running shorts and no pockets. Now turning to sit on the porch stoop, she decides to work it into her shoestrings, left running shoe. Looking down at Cat's picture while running will give me an incentive to keep going.

"I told her, and she remembered, that's so nice. Today is a long run, a ten miller at least two more of these before I move to the next level, Katherine says out loud to herself. As she is bending to attach the photo, she hears something coming up the front walk, heavy breathing, lopping, panting, large shadow ground level now quickly approaching.

"Hey big guy," she yells as she looks up." Did you sneak out again, Curtis? Bet your daddy doesn't know you are out and about."

Curtis comes right up to her, snuggles to her right leg, tail wagging, face smiling, ears down, licking away. The leg and running shoe fair game, a dog's tongue knows no bounds. Just about the same time Curtis is smelling and lapping away Katherine hears it, Mr. Powell a couple houses down the street.

"Curtis, Curtis, old boy come on, where the heck are you, you can't just roam the streets. Curtis come on boy, dinner time, dinner's ready." It's a familiar sound to Curtis. His ears pop up; apparently, he likes what he hears. He quickly shifts attention from Katherine's tasty legs, and he is off.

"See you buddy, until next time," Katherine says, turning her head to watch Curtis move on. He is quickly across the yard and headed home.

Katherine is focused again, working on attaching Cat's photo to her shoe. Just about done, giving a little tug to confirm, "Yep, all safe and secure," she says out loud and Bang, we are gone, Cat and me.

We crash land into the fixed garbage can next to the light pole on the corner. Quickly up, no madman, no truck in sight, thank God. Cat is taking inventory of herself and surroundings, both hands now grasping the rim of the barrel. Stabilizing herself and her thoughts, her mind clears a bit, realizing now she doesn't know where she is, and her bike is long gone. The truck, madman, and his maniacal ranting are a distant nightmare. In her mind flashes a distant snapshot of being at home, front porch, mom, Curtis, and her school picture. All there, from madman to mom to this corner, all of it like a fogged bathroom mirror before you wipe it clean. What the heck is going on, she is thinking shaking her head, right to left, left to right trying to wipe it all clean, clear. She feels a throb coming from her head now, reaching up to touch and rub the small knot on the back left hand side of her scalp. It is very sensitive. I hit my head; she is thinking. She remembers being thrown her into the truck, slamming against the door and cowering to the floorboard. Maybe that's where these weird thoughts come from.

"Pain's not too bad," she says out loud to herself, her left side also sore. Trying again to figure out where she is, the green roadway sign to the left indicates Deezavala Street, businesses and cars all around, Whataburger on the corner. It registers but not yet helping pinpoint her location. It registers with me that the pole is bent about bumper high, indicating this is where the truck landed. She takes a couple of deep breaths, does this again, back to holding on to the barrel with both hands. This time looking down into the trash, a computer print-out is staring her in the face. It registers, she knows this print-out is important and somehow connected to why she is here at this corner, at this moment in time. She reaches in, throws off Domino's pizza box and Diet Coke jug and grabs it, taking quick look at the computer paper. "Nothing interesting'" she folds it up. "Need to keep it," she says and toes to put it in her back pocket.

It doesn't fit. Her phone is in the way. Almost instantly she yells out loudly, "yes, way cool," as she pumps her arm and hand up and down. Her fisted hand still grasping the print-out and a deep sigh on her part, her shoulders now relax. Her phone is in the way, how cool is that she is joyfully thinking to herself. Her other hand now reaches around and behind, comfort, safety, and a way home in one small device. She grabs her phone with her free hand and Bang, I am gone.

Chapter Three

I land in Jules's room as this is where I started, but Jules is nowhere to be found. On her desk is Anna's box of stuff, what is left from her life besides Jules, but now no Ripfold in site. Immediately I think of Dan, we need Dan, I am thinking. I am back in Sharonville, but he is in San Antonio, Cat and Katherine are in San Antonio, Madman is likely still in San Antonio. I pull out my phone, find Dan's info and hit call, it rings and rings, no answer. I hang up before I can leave message too urgent for that so decide to text "Dan urgent something horrible happening in San Antonio happening right now PLEASE CALL," and hit send.

Now what to do I think, settling on edge of Jules's bed, in Jules room, upstairs alone. I don't know if her uncle is home. That's a problem because I can't just waltz out of here and wave at him as I walk by, so I text Jules. "In your bedroom-where are you?"

"Are you insane," she responds immediately. "My uncle will kill you, then me!

"Ripfold threw me back," I text.

"Lay low, don't make any noise if he comes upstairs jump out the window, be there in fifteen," her response.

The very second we disconnect, Dan's name pops up my screen, indicating I have a call and my phone lights up; green to answer, red to stop, hit red. Follow with a quick text:

"Sorry can't answer, dangerous. Just back from San Antonio, Ripfold. Mother and child in danger. Katherine and Cat Heard. No address. Katherine ex Girta Tech.

Madman after both. Madman in old Primate Plus truck, Ohio plates. Daughter gifted like Jules and I. Mother left for dead in creek bed," hit send.

Dan's response: "Katherine Heard found by a dog last news report still critical condition headlines from days ago, no mention of a daughter, call whenever safe."

Follow up text from Dan ten minutes later.

"Called office and then Googled; unrelated story to Katherine, truck found and impounded from accident scene. The truck was found close to where I live expired registration to Primate Plus. Police have contacted our office here is San Antonio. Shoes found inside on passenger side, one running shoe had child photo laced inside, small traces of blood. Police also found a damaged child's bike in the truck bed. No driver or owner has surfaced or come forward. Police asking for witnesses, asked Primates Plus to help with truck, otherwise, police not commenting."

My response: "the shoe photo is of Cat Heard, Katherine's daughter, the bike is also hers. She got away, at least for now. Will call soon."

Jules walks in, does not close the door, it's her room. She sits next to me. "Hi, she says welcome back," and kisses my left cheek. "My uncle's not home he left a note on kitchen table took an early shift at work," she says out loud. I hand her my phone so she can read the text exchange with Dan, thinking it's the quickest way to get her up to speed.

"Wow," is all she says.

"There is a lot going on in Texas."

We dial Dan and put him on speaker. Tell him this might take a while. He indicates he is settled in, fire away when ready. He is in a unique position, I am thinking. He is not one of us, but he knows and understands us. I warn him this might sound like a stream of Futurama sitcoms. He just laughs. This also creates kind of a, sticky wicket legally, I add, for Dan and Jules, but we need to discuss the legal implications some other time. Right now, the primary objective is to determine if Cat is safe.

Jules starts us off, tells Dan thank you for sending her mom's belongings, also tells him about the hitchhiking Ripfold in Anna's box. The Ripfold, she explains, was stubborn and came back a second time. Then she quickly described her own short fold trip inside Katherine to a local San Antonio brew pub to watch, among other things, a Spurs basketball game. Jules may at that time, she says, have met the bad guy through Katherine. Her only memory is having Katherine put the man's card in her back pocket then gone right after this action completed.

My turn. First, I want to tell Dan how happy I am Katherine was found and in good hands, but I follow quickly with Curtis and Katherine, jumping through all the detail because I am impatient to discuss Cat and the crazy man. We need to focus on Cat, I say, concerned about my second Ripfold trip Cat could be in great danger. She escaped, we escaped for now, but the madman is still out there, on the loose in Texas, in San Antonio. A deranged madman kidnapped us. I was in Cat through the Ripfold. There is no doubt in my mind that the madman meant deadly harm, clear violent intention on his part. What I thought was Cat's phone turned out to be Cat's Ripfold next to or near her phone. Her own Ripfold, not mine.

I continue describing to Dan that Cat's mother Katherine was a salesperson at Girta at or about the same time as Binky and Alcott. Cat is probably twelve maybe thirteen, mature for such a young age. She bravely went to grab her phone, and her hand pierced the Ripfold. She did not know what it was, this journey was her first. At the same time, we grabbed the Girta print-out. I believe Cat has the print-out now folded up in her own back pocket, wherever she might be.

Weirdly enough we, meaning Cat and I, were inside Katherine, her mother, I think for lack of a better term, a double Ripfold. Her fold memory was not mine, but I believe Cat's Ripfold memory was to remind her mom to take Cat's picture with her. Katherine was headed out for a run as she is training for another marathon. When she affixed this picture to her shoe, we were gone. This possession of the picture being the trigger or memory Cat was to restore, that is how I know the running shoe in the Madman's truck is Katherine's, securing a picture of Caty.

"I was gone out of Cat once she realized her phone was in her back pocket, but I believe the memory restore for my Ripfold was the computer print- out. We were thrown out of Cat's Ripfold at the scene of the truck crash into the light pole and next to a city trash barrel. While holding onto the barrel to gather her thoughts, she saw the print-out at the top of the litter basket. She grabbed it, recognizing it was what the madman had been waving around inside the moving truck. She discovered her phone in this process, and that is where and how I left her. Next to the light pole and trash barrel alone and armed with only a paper list of names and a small mobile phone," I say in disappointment.

For the first time now thinking to myself, I am likely on the list, the Girta print-out, maybe even Jules. Jules and I are still on call with Dan.

"Based on your text to me earlier today, Dan, I continue Katherine is in the hospital, almost certainly the result of the madman. Cat having escaped likely his current target; we know her mom is not at home and the madman does too. We can't go to the police with what we know. They would think us somehow involved, or guilty. It also sounds like the police are interested in the truck, having connected it with Primates. Dan, you are in the unique position of understanding us. Can you help us find Cat, at least help determine if she is safe?" I continue, "Once the police connect Cat and Katherine, she can tell the police what they need to know, she can connect the shoe, photo, bike, and truck. Once they hear of the attempted kidnapping, they will protect her, but this needs to happen fast, as soon as possible," I conclude, now out of breath and exhausted. I pause to look at Jules, neither of us with anything left to add.

After a brief pause, "That it, guys?" Dan asks.

"Yes sir," I respond.

"Okay, give me a little time to dig into this. I understand the seriousness and I will get back to you as soon as I find Cat."

"Thanks," Jules and I say simultaneously, as the call ends.

"Amazing what a little virus can do to common sense," Jimmy says to all of us, the four of us together for the first time in weeks now assembled at Ming's Chinese Street Food Diner. It is just a few days since my experience with Cat and the madman and I want to tell the group. Ming's has also finished translating *The Monkey's Paw*. Diane is also here, working tonight. Our team is assembled now, ready to get to work.

"A little deductive reasoning or logic might help you guys settle in a bit; want to hear what I think?" Jimmy says.

Jules, chiming in somewhat sarcastically more fun like, "Well this should be interesting."

Jimmy looks at her then the rest of us. "May I?" he formally requests approval, nods or smiles from all. Now with everyone's full attention he begins.

"Branded, you, Jules and others enter the person whose memory has been bent by the virus, to put things right. Dan told us when someone jumps into a Ripfold, their person and essence separate. Their Essence or true self is left behind when the person goes into the fold. Billy was one of you, a Folder maybe, an original like Branded and Jules. Dan knows Billy is inside him. He told us but more like his conscience now. Anna took three chimps with her, believing each had someone's essence. Each chimp presumably carried the essence of a Folder.

"Anna believed one of the chimps housed Billy's essence. Preferring the chimp, Billy over Dan the human. Two of the chimps were buried at Anna's compound. One headstone labeled Billy, a second labeled Sean. Sean's grave when found was said to be shallow, raided, and dug up by wild animals. The third chimp, KY, is alive. It is believed to contain Binky's essence. This chimp is now at the Cincinnati Zoo.

"The Texas Madman, as Branded refers to him, knows about Girta, Ripfolds, and the virus, clearly believing this to be the work of the devil.

"Finally, don't forget Brandon's own experience with Jeeves's essence. His essence desperately trying to reunite with Jeeves inside the Ripfold slams into Brandon to get inside the fold. This reunion briefly resulted in the emergence of the Findlay Crawler. We know or believe the Crawler exists but on the other side of the fold. Jeeves and the essence reunited as the Crawler would also know of Girta, Ripfolds, and the virus.

"Logically, therefore, this leaves two possibilities emanating from this set of facts or events: The Findlay Crawler found a way out, or whatever human Sean entered through his Ripfold is still alive, like Dan and Billy found a way out, Sean then may have raided the chimp's grave and reconnected with his essence. Now all three are possibly together again for the first time, a.k.a., the Texas Madman." As Jimmy pauses, I recall *The Monkey's Paw*, Ming's to tell us more tonight. In the Paw the son emerged from the dead, until his own parents' final wish sends him back!

"Now either or both the Texas Madman and the Findlay Crawler are deranged, gone mad, and looking for revenge," Jimmy finishes. I must admire Jimmy's flair for the dramatic. All of us, including me, are sucked in. He's created two bad guys and branded both simultaneously, move over WSJ Man, I am thinking.

"As crazy and preposterous as that sounds, I must admit it does follow a kind of demented logic," Jules says. "Maybe even some warped form of deductive reasoning, but logic and reasoning from a twisted fantasy or cartoon," she concludes.

"Not normal just logical, much easier for me to see since I am on the outside looking in," he says to all. Jimmy displays to the group his own form of human superpowers, I think to myself, although twisted and deranged superpowers, I think, laughing to myself.

Ming's looks to step into the conversation, anxious to do a quick download on *The Monkey's Paw*.

"Guys, I need to leave soon," he says. "I'm meeting Alcott in a bit, attempting to work through our differences and meeting at the warehouse. Trying to see if Alcott has any ideas about the Assembler computers. They were created under his watch, with his guidance, I thought I would also discuss the Combiner. The large 'one way,' Ripfold you guys uncovered at the Institute, as I am still puzzled about how it was moved from Dayton to Columbus."

Glad to hear that, I am thinking to myself as Ming's keeps pushing forward with the group.

"Jimmy's use of the three chimps is appropriate as background to Binky's use of *The Monkey's Paw*. If you think *For Whom the Bell Tolls* is Binky's initial instruction or guidance, you can think of *The Monkey's* Paw as her summary, the conclusion.

"Binky's message like the Paw itself is short and to the point, her message behind WW Jacobs's prose; the virus has unintended consequences, from those whose memory was altered, to the Folders whose memory is to fix. Like a Paw's wish, each turn has unintended consequences that cannot likely be anticipated. Just look how deep each of you has already traveled inside the Ripfold. Each with its own twists and turns with Katherine, Cat, Curtis, Jeeves, on and on! The journeys you have already taken are living evidence of her message and what she foresaw. She knew or came to believe each would be unique; each would serve a purpose. She also knew there would be trouble, even the possible emergence of evil; The Findlay Crawler, the Texas Madman, others yet discovered, who knows," Ming's finishes and gets up to leave.

"I need to leave and drive to the warehouse downtown, will send a complete translation of the Paw once complete, should be worth reading. One final thought before I leave, there is more," he indicates to all of us. "We have the literal beginning and end of Binky's research. There is clearly much in between left to discover. It might be locked up in the warehouse computers, might be somewhere else, possibly more dime store novels yet to be found," Ming's says, now looking directly at me, holding the gaze much longer than needed. Then he says goodbye and heads out to meet with Alcott. I hear what he is saying, I know there is more, more in the attic now guessing more in Anna's box.

Ming's understands this; he also understands not discussing in public even amongst the group, there is a good reason Binky went to all that trouble, a reason she hid her work.

Ming's is now gone and it's just Jules, Jimmy, and me at the diner. As Diane approaches the table to see what we might need, Jimmy indicates he was not quite finished before. Looking at us now, wondering if he might take a few more moments of our time, Jules nods with hands and arms extended, indicating he has the floor. Once again panning the booth, he seems happy it is just Jules and me while establishing direct eye contact with both of us. Momentarily he settles on me.

"Of course," he begins, "if you follow my logic with the great apes there is another possibility, another trail that may have emerged, that might exist. There is an obvious hole or event in my logic, in my thinking, one additional prospect to emanate from the three chimps," Jimmy once again has our full attention. "Billy is inside Dan, Billy's essence dead and buried, chimp and human #1 accounted for. Sean, the Texas Madman, may have emerged and reunited with his essence, chimp and human #2 discovered, although not yet identified," Jimmy says, looking at us. "Binky's essence is believed to be inside KY at the Cincinnati Zoo, pointing us to chimp #3," Jimmy stops, watching both of us.

Jules jumps in before Jimmy can fire back up.

"You think Binky may be alive and walking around in human form, human #3, having somehow emerged from a Ripfold? Is that where this is headed?" she says. Jimmy, being respectful, knowing this is my mom, turns to look at me.

"Yes," he says, slowly and deliberately, "And believe I know who it is."

Chapter Four

Only a few hours since we hung up with Dan, walking around Jules's neighborhood now, but there's not much to see. We're not paying much attention, but one thing for certain the area around her home has many challenges. The clouds, heat, and humidity slow us down, weigh us down even more when my phone lights up, the only sunshine of the day.

Text from Dan, "Cat is good, safe with Katherine's mother as you guessed, police treating it as kidnapping. Came down hard on Primates because of truck registration. Company put me in charge. Police have APB out for the driver. They have very little to go on, nothing really."

The sticky wicket I referred to earlier, I am thinking to myself. No way to know what the madman looks like; I live in Cincinnati. It would be hard to explain to the police or to anyone for that matter except for Jules or Dan. I do recall something just as we entered Cat's Ripfold during a brief flash of eye contact when we grabbed the computer print-out, something familiar, something unsettling to me but very familiar. Then I describe this moment to Jules, the look, but nothing I can grasp, nothing I can describe just yet with any certainty.

I Text Dan: "Recall, the madman was large, my guess 6'3" and over two hundred pounds, white male aggressively strong, brownish hair, not thick or much. Guess also in his thirties, mid to older, guess again righthanded. The way he flung us easily to far side of the truck." hit send.

"Thanks," Dan responds." Gives me a little something to work with even if I can't go to the police. With Cat in custody and

Katherine gaining strength, guessing madman is digging in deep somewhere, maybe even moving on."

"Possibly," my return text, "but he needs the computer print-out. He can't terrorize the Girta crowd without it," I text back.

"It was an original," I say, turning to face Jules as we move along the street headed back to her house, "The computer print-out was not a copy, and I don't think he has another. I doubt he made a copy as it was one continuous piece, I know that from when he threw it at us. Madman didn't strike me as the plan-ahead type, more the shoot, aim, and load type. We can only hope he has little or no access to the database or machines that produced it," I say to Jules.

Then we decide to end the text chain with Dan, "Thanks for follow up Dan. Good to know Cat is safe. Please let us know how Katherine does and what else you find."

Now looking at Jules as we approach her front door, "We can't lose site of the business card," I say. "The card that spurred your exit from Katherine's Ripfold likely is still in her back pocket. We may be the only ones that know that link exists. Maybe just what we need to expose the Texas Madman. There is one thing I know for certain, thinking out loud to Jules, I am certain we need Dan. We need him as a part of our team. He has a bad guy created by a Ripfold in his backyard and you and I here in Ohio."

Jules chimes in as we are standing on her front porch, "Don't forget Cat, she is one of us, Katherine might be as well, they might both be folders and there may be others like them in and around San Antonio. Cat may not remember or realize it yet, and she may write it off to a bump on the head, but they won't go away. The virus is persistent, the Ripfolds will keep coming and she will need someone to help her understand. You had me, I had Ming's, she has only us and maybe Dan," Jules finishes.

"Alcott bought the building," Ming's tells me.

"What building?" I ask.

"Mine, ours, the warehouse, this warehouse, this building, my home. More importantly he believes he controls the Assemblers, although control is probably the wrong word. He believes he owns the central computer from which the Assemblers' knowledge exists, but he has no idea how this might occur as he does not know how they function or operate; he also believes the computers along the wall here may be linked as a part of the original project protocol."

"Wow," is all I can say in return.

"One other thing he is responsible for the Combiner, its ongoing existence and moving it to Columbus many years ago. Finally, maybe most importantly, he believes you have a special gift, pointing to the rapid discovery by you, Julia, and Jimmy, the history and events you have uncovered, makes sense," he says. "You are Binky's son," Ming's concludes.

It's been a few days since the team meeting at the diner. Ming's is catching me up on his meeting with Alcott later that same night.

The mention of Jules and Jimmy reminds me Jimmy dropped me off, and I am here alone here to visit Ming's. Jimmy is heading to the zoo. He has a date. Jules at home, "not feeling well-girly thing," she said. We were supposed to double-date like other teens. Our first, my first I assume Jules's first double date, but this thought strikes me as funny. I don't really know what she was doing before us, before me and before we met at the Study Place. We never really talk about stuff like that. I'm beginning to wonder what other kids talk about. Maybe they just hang out and talk about silly, goofy everyday things, I am thinking. This thought reminds me that it is time to get back to basketball. The head coach has been reaching out and I miss the running, pushing, shoving, and constant back and forth on court.

"You okay?" Ming's says. He can tell I am distracted.

"Yes sorry. I was wondering how many sixteen-year-olds are doing what I'm doing today."

Ming's hears my complaint and laughs, "Well, that is a chain of thought best to avoid," he speaks." For what it is worth, I often used to wander the same thing. I went through high school by thirteen did not get to kiss a girl not even close, never held someone's hand, never saw a football game. Never snuck out at night or caused any trouble, just studied and worked, study and work."

"Damn," I say aloud, "And here I am complaining to you."

"I watch you guys," Ming's continues, "you, Jules, and Jimmy and sometimes wonder what it's like, once again me living on the outside looking in." Remembering now what Jimmy said at dinner last week, different context, same words.

"Things are better for me now," Ming's indicates. "I understand more, did not really know how to talk to others back then. College was similar but better. I was closer to others, closer to normal. I could sit in the Student Commons area, which I did, often. I was young then but it did not seem to matter much, blended well watching sports and gamers. I did not understand them but watched and listened to others, even laughing with others from a distance most of the time I did not know what was funny but still felt good. They started playing video games in the Commons as my route to normal. There was a train of couches all around the outer edges. The kids would hang out all weekend and late night into the week. It didn't really matter who was there, all of us just playing video games on the monitors. There were monitors on the wall and controllers thrown all over the place. Finally, picked one up turned the games on and I was off, the video games became my bridge to normal. Well, I guess normal, I was only sixteen at the time," he ends. We just sit for a couple of minutes, no need to rush its Saturday afternoon, neither of us going anywhere.

"What do you think we should do about Alcott," Ming's asks.

"How the hell should I know," I say quicker and louder than justified, "You're the child genius," I say in my defense. We both look at each other for a single second of silence or less then burst into laughter. The more we look at each other the harder we laugh.

We can't stop, and this goes on for minutes. Finally, Ming's breaks the hold. "I need to take in some oxygen," he squeaks out and the laughter now slowly running its course.

"Can we go eat," he finally manages to say with the laughter still leaving a trail just behind his voice." I am starving," he says.

"No argument from me let's get out of here, Mainliner," I half ask.

Alcott has aged, looks older, something beyond tired. It's probably been a little less than a month since I last saw him. In any event, the road is now leading back to Alcott, so we are gathered again at the Mainliner in our old table. This time Jimmy and I on the back side of booth, facing Jules and Ming's, Alcott slides in next to them a few minutes after we arrive. Now the three of them are facing us and the outside parking field. He has been active for sure, buying the building, meeting with Ming's, research and emails and who knows what else, guessing we will find out today? Like it or not, he has become part of the group. I am personally undecided but tend to give everyone the benefit of the doubt; it's my nature. However, he is sneaky and has inserted himself uninvited numerous times. He often seems to be on his own mission, so I hope to hear more about that today. Jules is skeptical, I know, but carries an obvious soft spot for him.

With little hesitation, Mr. Alcott starts. He is used to being in charge.

"Good to see each of you again," he says. "I appreciate your agreeing to meet with me. Life has a funny way of coming around. So here we are again. As Peter has likely told you, I bought the warehouse building. I did this for a reason, of course I do most things for a reason, it's my nature. I believe but don't know the computers in the building, the row of computers along the front wall contains important history but also believe they may have inside them all the basic research and background to the Girta virus project. More importantly they might disclose how Brandon and Julia can do what you do," as he shifts his focus back and forth to me then Jules.

"I should back up," Robert says. "I'm getting ahead of myself again, confession in order, history is important. I was a part of the team, in fact the nucleus surrounding Binky's research. By team, I mean Binky, Paul, Anna, Peter myself and a few others, including the Girta MIS director at the time who has been instrumental in understanding and accessing the Assembler mechanisms of which you are aware. We can discuss this in more detail today."

Alcott now leans forward and then right to see and look directly at Jules, "Julia, I did not know you were Anna's daughter, how could I? However, I will admit this single link became my incentive to reinvest myself in the past, now this present. It may not be apparent to the four of you, but this decision is very painful for me. Binky's research changed my life in more ways than you will ever know."

Lunch arrives, Mr. Alcott, preferring not to order, requests we eat and let him continue.

"Works for me," Jimmy says and all we dig in while Robert continues.

"The Girta contracted project was initially labeled Acute Behavioral Disorganization a Result of the Trauma of War and other Violent Events Resulting in Decreased Combatant Fighting Efficiencies, clearly a mouthful," he says as Jimmys chomps down on half his sandwich. "In short, we were to develop a treatment for PTSD, Post-Traumatic Stress Disorder. The Girta internal code name for the project was Shell Shock. I believe Peter or Mings has given you much of the background for this project. Binky's initial work was extraordinarily successful. The Department of Health and Lead Contractor for the IDIQ were very excited, increasing awards and funding for the project numerous times in the first year and we ended up with eleven government funded fingers or offshoots. All these somewhat or directly related to the original contracted purpose and scope. This is one of the reasons we purchased Chemie Research company, bringing in the Huang's," Robert briefly looks and nods at Mings to acknowledge this.

"Paul Huang, Mings dad like Binky, was known to be brilliant in the key research area. One of the development opportunities was internal to Girta, the last one started about two years after the original award and funded by some of our internal cash. My recollection is Binky called the work Object Event Viral Research; we called the project Battle Fatigue. The five of us sitting here today, I believe, are a direct result of project Battle Fatigue."

Robert continues, "Your mother, Brandon, used to call the things folds, tears or rips, as I recall, like a bedsheet on a clothesline with a tear, cut, or rip," she would say, "flowing freely to the wind. The tear rippling somewhat independently to the movement of the sheet with its own force and control, emanating a glow or warmth, the glow coming in waves toward or at her. More at her, I think, but that could be my own impression. I did not and could not see these rips, so my only understanding came through Binky. In all honesty, at first, I thought maybe she had an eye problem, possibly even the beginning of a serious medical disorder. Well, I was grounded in reality back then, knew, or believed everything had a logical explanation. Of course, I also had a company to run, and Binky was my chief scientist. If her sight or sanity was in question, if she was fading physically in any way, the research and, therefore, the awards and funding could be threatened or questioned. We had more than doubled our payroll to meet the demands of the project and Girta was now on everyone's radar, everyone at least in the government contracting space. A bright future," he says with weak enthusiasm, maybe even sadness.

"As a scientist she was fascinated by them, the rips or cuts at first, we didn't understand them or maybe I should say she didn't understand them. Around me or maybe because of me she did not approach or attempt to grab one of the folds or cuts, just seemed content to observe. Scientific principle was important to her. I do not know when she started entering these folds, I know eventually she did.

"Mings tells me you and Jules refer to the folds or cuts as Ripfolds, like cuts or wounds in the sky or ground," he asks invitingly while looking between the two of us." I will refer to them as Ripfolds to keep it simple."

Jules wants to join in. "Mr. Alcott, to take the conversation a step further, Ming's refers to me as a Linker, he says I convert computer object code to executable files and this action, according to Ming's, links the instruction to the action.

"Then Brandon arrives, the Loader, his job to deliver the executable files to the main memory. The restored memory can now unfold or happen as originally intended before the viral infection affected memory in the host." Alcott, looking at Jules, starts to chuckle a bit, not quite a laugh. "You know Julia there are not many people you could say that to," he says, "and not think you more than a little off center, but to me and the rest of us sitting here sounds normal."

"Well Peter here," as Robert nods his head in Ming's direction once again, "would know more about the computerese than I would. In my vernacular you are a Fixer or what the Battle Fatigue project labeled Fixers. Battle Fatigue had three stated objectives, or maybe I should say Binky had three stated objectives for the project Battle Fatigue; Contain, Fix, and Prevent.

"Remember," Robert says, looking between and at all three of us, "at this point project Shell Shock was deep into research and development with over a hundred people and four locations in various labs around the United States. The largest most concentrated in Cincinnati with a large presence in San Antonio. The virus was out and uncontrollable, each of us a part of project Battle Fatigue was infected. That is why the final project team was so small. We wanted to try and minimize the impact to each of us. Each of the team members and their families was affected in different ways, no real pattern to follow or to guide us to help define Binky's objective of Contain.

"Containing the impact of what the project created and unleashed was more difficult than we imagined, thus ultimately our answer or response was to shut it down. This solution was not easy for me as there were possibilities a part of the program that could be life changing, world changing potentially from large financial rewards to power and control. Some other time I will elaborate, but for now, enough to disclose that the Department of Defense got involved. Two of the program offshoots I mentioned before went in a dark direction. Some of us, including myself, sucked into the sheer magnitude and power of it, enough said.

"Julia, back to the question. You are a direct result of the second objective; to fix the damage we did. Hundreds of memories were already broken, more and more Ripfolds appearing every day. At least that is what Binky and Anna were telling us. We or more specifically I had no way of knowing this to be true. Again, Mings knows more of the basic science behind what occurred, so please feel free to jump   in," he says, nodding in his direction.

"As I understand it, Binky, then as a part of her Object Event Viral program, created a variant to the existing virus then coupled this with her mRNA background. At some point Binky went rogue and she and Anna self-experimented. Anna became the first real Loader. They then essentially accessed the Ripfolds to send Loaders back to restore memory files. I have no clue how this could have been achieved. From what I could tell, Binky kept no notes, at least none that we ever found. I can tell you we searched long and hard, bringing in forensic specialists and experts from around the world.

This was my personal attempt to circumvent Binky's demand to close the program. My alternative plan was to have Paul Huang, Peter's father, replace Binky and keep the projects rolling forward, at least certain aspects of the projects. However, we didn't get very far because Binky somehow found a way to hide or contain all her work." Robert finishes now, needing a minute to breathe and rest.

"In any event, Julia, you are clearly Anna's daughter," Robert, having now caught his breath, begins again. "Finally, let me address the third element, the third stage, the final stage; the Prevent. The Prevent stage of the project did not really occur until years later once the DOD had decided to abort and abandon the project.

"Based on what Peter tells me, you know and have seen the Compiler, which is directly linked to the Assemblers. Together the Compiler and the Assemblers make up the find, contain, and destroy the virus and everything a part of it--the Prevent function. The Prevent objective was to clean up and end the program forever.

"Fast forward to the present for reasons I don't fully understand, almost ten years later I have made it my personal mission to oversee and maintain stage three. As Peter knows, I am responsible for oversight of the central computer to the Assemblers, moving and maintaining the Compiler in Columbus, funding the care and upkeep of a certain bonobo chimp and now the purchase of Peter's building and computers, go figure," he ends.

"Robert," I ask getting his attention, "you mention three locations other than Cincinnati, one of these as San Antonio, is there a reason you chose San Antonio?" I ask.

Without any hesitation he replies, "Yes, in fact there were three very specific reasons; The Texas Biomedical Research Institute where we officed and collaborated for a period, The Southwest National Research Center and the affiliated Primate Service Research Center, which gave us instant accredited access to the labs and equipment we needed and, of course, our primate supplier specifically Bonobo Monkeys. Finally, maybe most importantly, and I guess reason number four, Robert Jr., my son, was willing to move and open our office in San Antonio. He was instrumental in the Prevent Objective I alluded to earlier. He lives in South Texas to this very day."

Chapter Five

Alcott is on the phone with his son.

"How's mom doing," he asks.

"Well, you know pretty much the same as always, good and overall, still hanging in there. Hasn't changed, her appetite is still good, eats like a horse and still gets feisty if dinner doesn't arrive on time. Guessing she has seen every Hallmark movie more than a few times."

"That would make anyone feisty," Robert Jr. says and laughs." Wish her happy mom's day for me please," he asks, "even if she won't know it's me?"

"Yes, yes will do, did that this morning, couple of times but will do again for good measure. Doctor is always reminding me to keep things normal, keep it day to day, like it was." That comment causes Robert and his son to stop, each remembering Pat and mom in their own way. The old Pat, the old mom.

It takes a few minutes, but Robert Sr. asks, "How you been, how's work, busy?"

"Good, really good," Jr. responds. "I wanted to ask you, had something else to ask you," Jr., says.

"About?" Robert Sr. quickly returns.

"Well, I have had a few memory lapses lately kind of grown in length really, I know with mom it's cancer, more definable, easier to understand and treat. Hate to rehash old issues but any guidance? Do you still have issues blacking out?" his son asks.

"Did you?" His dad responds." Black outs, long periods of time?" Sr. adds quickly, "Not more often, but longer, darker, little or no recollection?" Jr. responds.

Robert Sr. can't answer because it's hard to breathe; he know it's the virus and doesn't want to consider the consequences. His breathing now labored, shallow, probably drained of color, feeling faint, hands clammy, pushing phone hard against his own head. The pressure of the phone feels good; hoping he doesn't black out while talking with his only son.

All team members are present and accounted for but Mr. Robert T. Alcott. Back to Ming's Chinese Street food diner in Evandale. Diane is also missing in action tonight. We hope she has a date. We know she lives alone; "no children," she told us except of course "the two of you." I know she likes to say, meaning Jules and me.

Last week was the meeting with Mr. Alcott. Right now, Jimmy and Ming's kiddingly going back and forth while Jules and I sort of listen in. Jimmy practicing his branding ideas, wants to know if Ming's would prefer being known as Ming's "the mad scientist" or "mad-man-Ming's." Not sure this is a new handle or just Jimmy. I don't think anyone has asked Ming's until now. Ming's called us together to update the team on a few items, probably now wants to change his name. Appears to be favoring or leaning toward the mad man moniker. It makes him sound "badass," he tells Jimmy while laughing. Jules and I enjoying the debate.

"Never been a badass before," Ming's jokingly says.

We settle in and Ming's wants to cover a few things Alcott did not address during last week's visit. He said they were important enough to come back together.

"Alcott has moved the Assemblers' main frame computer to the warehouse. I have not hooked it up yet or even plugged it in. I have some concerns. He has also sent me a lease to rent the warehouse space in case something happens to him, meaning to Alcott," he continues. "One dollar a year rent, I pay all expenses, much less than

I am paying now," Ming's says. "As part of the offer, he has set up an Ohio based not for profit company, The Huang Institute, Alcott's name choice not mine," Ming's is quick to point out. "Additionally, Robert indicated a willingness to invest a significant amount of his own money as well as helping to raise capital for future R&D." Ming's, finished for now, takes a drink and is now looking at me.

Robert is clearly inserting himself again, I think to myself. Not sure if this is good or bad. Jules wants to know what Ming's thinks, pointing out she is just sixteen and has no experience in this type of stuff. Jimmy and I are in the same position, I add.

"Let us begin with the computers," Ming's says. "You will recall what Robert said two of the contracted programs were with the Department of Defense, but he used the term DOD. My dad and I were part of both research programs, to a point. In fact, a DOD assigned science team controlled the program from an undisclosed Maryland office. The DOD focus, for lack of better explanation, was to manipulate memory, maybe controlling memory more accurately, but essentially attempting to control the thoughts of others. Alcott was the central point person for Girta and all DOD communication. We reported only to him, talked to no one else, including Binky, kept highly confidential, program labeled Top Secret-Compartmented, the highest level of U. S. security clearance. We, meaning my dad and I, were given very specific instructions delivered in two legal-size blue folders. These folders were delivered by Alcott the first Monday of every month. Each file had a name. The program names: Gedachtnis and die Erinnerung, the German terms for memory. The German language has two words to represent memory.

I don't speak German, my understanding is not deep so bear with me; Gedachtnis is the collection of past knowledge, the facts, or data, Erinnerung is the reproduction or recollection of knowledge. In our vernacular, Gedachtnis is the computer hard drive, Erinnerund the file, triggering or opening the file. It was the DOD answer to addressing the Linker and Loader functions created by

Binky. Each of these programs were linked to the Assembler computers and ultimately to the Compiler. My dad and I referred to them as "Geda" and "Erin," our children. In fact, it was just too frustrating to fully pronounce the two words every day.

"I am concerned that booting Geda and Erin back up could have real consequences. There could be a link, signal, or tracker back to the DOD, letting them know the program is live again. This could bring someone back to Cincinnati, back to Girta and ultimately back to us. In addition, the combination of the mainframe and warehouse computers could very well house Binky's research. I don't think these machines have ever been linked before. Remember we only have the beginning and the end from Binky's notes, *For Whom the Bell Tolls* to *The Monkey's Paw*, everything in between missing."

"Finally," Alcott looms, "raising the project from the dead could change everything. He knows more about these two files and the entire program than anyone alive, who knows what stirs inside him like a real-life Monkey's Paw," he says nervously." Ming's finishes and needs a break after drinking a little water and a few minutes for him to breathe.

I ask, "Is this experience with the DOD program the reason you do not trust Alcott?"

"Yes," he responds instantly, "but in fairness I believe now he is very different person. Different in more ways than one. In the old days he never took no for an answer, in the past he never accepted any deviation or change unless, of course, it came from him. He was obsessed; my dad used to say possessed. However, I believed him yesterday when he said that reliving Binky's work very painful to him, Ming's recants, and that the virus experience dramatically changed his life," Ming's continues before any of us respond." He and his entire family were infected. I've not heard recently but believe his wife never fully recovered," Ming's states and finishes.

Not sure why we are here. I have not been to a funeral since Binky died. I was just a kid back then. Maybe because I am sixteen, but this seems like a total waste of time.

However, here, we are, Jules, Jimmy, and me together again because Mr. Alcott's wife died. Ming's recent reference to her being sick turned quickly dark. We didn't know her, never saw her not even a picture, but understood she had been sick for a long time. Robert hasn't been around for the last few weeks. It probably got very hard for him. Ming's felt like we should be here. He is in the middle of the church somewhere we believe to the far side of the building. He indicated that the virus linked to her death, Alcott believing it triggered the cancer, it just took the cancer awhile to come around. Finally found its way in the end and that's why we are here. We are in the very back of a large cathedral at a service called the last rights mass, in a Catholic church at a Catholic mass. A lot of muttering to me, can't really hear much as the priest speaks. Maybe if you knew the verse, many of the people here are moving their lips, clearly knowing what the priest will say next. Looking around, Catholics go all in for symbols surrounded by icons, figures, and statues like mummies with faces, one on every corner, in every nook and cranny. We have been here for an hour now.

It appears service may be coming to an end, hopefully now over as priest moves from behind the altar to center stage, arms spread, now mimicking a couple of the statues. At least he is not looking up, I am thinking, like the statue to the right of me he does, however, look at Robert and nod. With this action a man in a gold jacket, part of Catholic service team, comes over to invite the family to stand and move out. Robert and his family are up and now moving toward the aisle. I am quickly up and starting to scoot into the far-left side away from the procession that has started, but Jules grabs my arm.

"Can't," she whispers to me, "have to let the family and friends pass first." We are in the last row and the last few seats in the last row. Immediately, one of my dad's favorite lines comes to mind; "last in last out." When I showed up late for dinner, he would say, "learn to be on time." His lecture would continue, "True in accounting, true in life, last in last out." Now I know true at funerals as well. We are last to exit the church a good fifteen minutes later.

Now in the car and headed to the burial, nothing to say as the three of us drove along. So, we are just following the many cars. I would rather not go to reception, thinking to myself I don't know a soul except Ming's and Robert, free food is just not enough incentive even for a teenager.

"Not sure why we are going to a burial lowering a big box into a hole?" I say out loud to Jules and Jimmy.

"Not really," Jules says.

"Not really what?" I ask.

"The priest just says a prayer over the casket then everyone leaves, the box into the whole thing is for the movies, not really done anymore, they do that later now maybe even tomorrow depending on weather," she indicates.

"Well hang in there," Jimmy chimes in, "the burial thing goes fast, most people anxious to get to the free food and drink. I went to my uncle's burial last year, it took less than a few minutes. In and out like the burger place and had a blast at the reception, even got two or three beers down before my dad caught on. Felt terrible later that same day," he says, reminiscing.

"All right well that sounds better, much better," I respond.

"What, you like to see me suffer?" Jimmy pleads. A little laughter from all of us and we relax a bit as we have now entered and are snaking our way into the cemetery property with the rest of the cars. The procession makes a couple of turns and stops now like one big, organized pile up, everyone just pulling over and parking.

At least it's nice and sunny outside. I wonder what they do if it's raining, I think to myself as we park and emerge to a beautiful area with large rolling, grassy hills, and occasional tree for shade. Then I noticed them. It sneaks up on you, neatly packaged into organized rows, burial plots, graves, and headstones, like a maze. They kind of disappear into the landscape, almost an illusion. We are now outside and starting to navigate with the crowd, but we are on the berm along the road with the grave sites to our right.

The field extending as far as you can see up the hill, one marker after another. Many of the graves have a little something left behind unique things along with the fresh flowers. I see one with a baseball glove and ball, another with a faded red hair burette. As we get closer, I can see Robert in the distance up front of the crowd, the first car behind the hearse, but we are still way back, guessing maybe fifty cars. I have grown to like him. Jules does too. He seems genuine, at least to us.

Of course, Jimmy has his own ideas about Robert, and we need to be careful discounting Jimmy's ideas. In my experience he is often right. In the distance a bell tolls. All three of us hear it. All three shuffle to a stop, each in our own diminished space.

Something eerily solemn permeates the air. Three times it's rung, maybe one for each of us, then I remember Mr. Hemingway's prose, "the bell tolls for every man…the bell tolls for thee." Before long the ring becomes a distant echo. We start back up and now I can see the rest of Robert's family out and gathered around a large black Cadillac.

Remember he told Jules and me, one daughter and a son but seems like six or seven people bunched together. Of course, we don't know or recognize any of them. Pall bearers now gathered around the hearse, all friends and family, Jules tells me and now removing a large white, ornate casket with bronze handles. In the distance I can also see a short stubby platform green velvet trim sitting on the ground just a few feet from the roadway to the right but on our side of the drive. The casket is now covered with a rose cluster sitting atop the stubby platform, ball bearers back to gather their own family and loved ones. We decide to approach from the grassy area, twenty or so feet into the knoll, proceeding single file in and around the many grave sites but making good time. Walking through a graveyard, a little tricky narrow path, thinking to myself, and there are graves on each side of the path. No real walkway, rows of headstones to the left and burial sites to the right. I assume head to the front and feet down, the dead and buried that is, seems logical. I am careful to lead us closer to the headstone side along the path. I don't want to step on any of the deceased's feet, belly, or face. That idea is really playing with my mind. Then I hear Jimmy in the back breaking the silence.

"Guys," he says, "pretty sure we are in the produce section."

"What?" Jules asks." Produce section, what does that mean," she repeats.

"You know fresh…" before Jimmy can get it out Jules figures it out and answers with a low-level scream, "You are such a sick person, that is so gross." As she lets go of the word gross, she also let's go of her arm, swinging at him Jimmy, way ahead of her and holding his ground a few feet back as he watches her arm smack nothing but air. People in the street looking our way but everyone is still moving steadily forward, I am just shaking my head at Jimmy and Jules. The street area reminds me of an audience gathering for a small jazz concert, slow, quiet, and deliberate. Just missing blankets, small chairs, and few bottles of wine needed to complete the picture. We are all making our way toward the casket and within a few minutes the entire crowd is gathered and loosely assembled. The three of us are perched on a shaded hill and grassy area looking down somewhat on the congregation. We can see Ming's a few rows back on the street. His earlier text to me, "going to reception?" I have not responded. The priest now closer to us on the casket head side with Robert and his two kids gathered at the foot end. Robert looks and acknowledges us with a warm smile and half hand wave then turns to his daughter and whispers in her ear. She looks up also with a smile and wave, then Robert to his son standing to the left. His son looks first at Jules. I can't blame him. I would do the same thing. He looks a lot like Robert, I am thinking. A couple inches taller, many pounds thicker but same handsome face just fewer lines. When he looks at me, I freeze, a chill hitting hard and fast Jr. looking directly at me. He also seems to freeze. We are both locked now, just staring at each other, I see him, he sees me, his eyes wide and straining with a blank dark stare. Something familiar very familiar for both of us, passing between us, I know who or what he is. The printout, the Girta print out, the old truck and Cat all come rushing back. Then we hear it, "let us pray," the priest says loudly, breaking the silence and our locked gaze, his arms fully outstretched palms pushed forward as if to calm everyone and this time looking skyward.

Chapter Six

Jimmy, wanting to start a conversation asks, "What kind of guy are you?"

I can only guess where this is headed, and it won't be good for my health, I am thinking but smiling. Jules, he, and I are heading to the warehouse to see Ming's. It's been couple of days since the funeral I have the paperback novel, *The Thirty-Nine Steps* by John Buchan with me for Ming's to decode.

Jules has it now in the back seat, reading the World War I dime store novel from Binky's box in the attic. Following up on Ming's unsaid but pointed reference, pointed at me.

"There is more," Ming's said, "much more to Binky's research."

With Jimmy, however, I decided best to play it safe. My response to his leading question, "I'm a Jules type guy," I say loudly with emphasis on "Jules." Jimmy is clearly disgusted by my response,

"You mean a brown nose type guy," more like it he quicky replies. Jules briefly looks up with a smile on her face. Jimmy, as is typical, continues without any prompting.

"Well for me, I'm more of a butt guy. You know, it is well known from the scientific literature that butt guys are very well rounded," he says looking at me stupid grin on his face, me left to shaking my head. Another set up, I am thinking to myself, "Freud, for one, was very clear on that," says Jimmy before I can respond.

"What do you know about Freud, you don't know squat about Freud," my reply, "One of my favorite authors, Agatha Freud, read all of her murder mysteries," says Jimmy now laughing out loud to himself.

"You're the only mystery around here," I fire back now, both of us laughing along together, Jules wisely chooses to sit this one out.

She is attempting to read *The Thirty-Nine Steps,* not sure how. I can't read in a moving car. It tends to make me sick. I have personally never read the book, but I know the story backwards and forwards, Ron read it to me over and over when I was very little. At night while in bed he would climb in next to me so we could read together just like his dad did before him. Of course, we also watched the Hitchcock produced movie series, helping bring the story to life, the movies and the book not always on the same page. Sherlock Homes, James Bond, and Obi Wan Kenobi all wrapped up into one; the one and only Richard Hannay, the main character in *The Thirty-Nine Steps*.

My recollection of the story starts at the end of a performance by, "Mr. Memory" a popular performer in his day. Uncanny ability remember he never forgets, perfect recollection and accompanying quick wit. That night performing at popular London music hall, Mr. Hanay, in attendance, meets an American, Franklin P. Scudder. Mr. Scudder admits to Hannay he is a freelance spy. He also admits having faked his own death but is clearly very much alive, claiming now to have information foreign agents want, information very important to national security. Hannay, believing him, allows Scudder to stay in his flat, but the very first night the spy is stabbed to death. Hannay then goes on the lam, believing he will be accused of the crime.

Our Mr. Hannay, however, is very cunning, skilled, and avoids capture, staying free to prove his innocence and save the country from a German spy ring, a group trying to bring down the British government. What are the thirty-nine steps? The book leads us to actual steps from a remote Lodge to the beachhead. Mr. Hitchcock's movie's a different twist, but either way it is here the final mystery will unfold, murder will be solved, and country saved, all by the hands and mind of Richard Hannay. Well, at least that's how this seven-year-old remembers it, the book and story line that is. It'll be interesting to see what Jules thinks.

Jules is giving me space but knows something is amuck. I plan to tell she and the team today about Robert Jr. I believe him to be the Texas Madman. Following Jimmy's logic, the result of Sean and his essence reunited inside Robert Alcott Jr.; human and essence #2 now accounted for and identified. The look we exchanged at the funeral was unforgettable. I've seen it twice now; once in the old truck as Cat, once two days ago at the funeral. How he can see me through Cat's eyes remains a mystery, but I believe he did, and we both now know. Which means the game is on. What game, I think to myself sarcastically. I know and saw what he did to Katherine, his intent with Cat. If a game, its cat and mouse and one of life and death.

Good news this week from Dan indicating Katherine is recovering. She was strong when Jr. hit; no doubt, she will carry scars beyond the obvious but it appears she and Cat are safe for now. The other concern. #2 likely has access to Girta information through Robert Sr., meaning he can probably duplicate the employee listing. He also saw both Jules and Jimmy, the three of us together at the burial and Jules clearly registered with him if he links me with the devil, he will likely draw a thick brush to the two of them.

It is not that unusual for Jules to get uninvited late-night visitors as the neighborhood where she lives breeds trouble. It doesn't happen often, but it happens enough. Her uncle, an iron worker, often works the midnight shift, usually at the old Body by Fischer plant and now the Fisher Industrial Park in the Village of Fairfield. The company rumored to have supplied some of the iron rods to build the Statue of Liberty. The building is like an unpulled long bow fronting the infamous Dixie Highway also known as Route 4 in Cincinnati, the old plant having put its stamp on thousands of General Motors cars and trucks, "Body by Fischer."

A light sleeper by necessity, she knows the sounds of her home. Something new, something different coming from the kitchen the door leading to the back porch, an easy mark. Last time this happened she fixed the door jamb before her uncle got home. In any event, she knows the drill, quickly up out of bed, gently grabs her phone slides into her chanclas then across the floor and into the closet. More sounds coming from down under, intruder now probably into the hallway but not yet to the stairs. Typically, they rummage through the foyer looking for something of value. Good luck, she mumbles lightly to herself. Whoever it is coming is now slightly closer, clumsy in a way, likely young, novice, or strung-out. None of these things are good for her, dangerous, probably both nervous, and stupid. Not much time but she knows the drill. She used to practice when she was younger, just not recently. An attic crawl space inside and over her closet can't be reached without the aid of a ladder, unless, of course, you know better. Built-in shelving on both sides of the inner closet wall deliberately kept empty, important footholds. Now she grabs the closet hanger bar with her right hand, uses it for leverage to lift her left foot to the second shelf far wall then her left hand to nailed post about six feet high, center stage for hats and jackets, raises last foot off the ground crawls spider woman style one more lift when left hand reaches up and pushes wooden flap off to the left. Can't hear anything from prowler now, she is too deep into the closet, does not know his status. She does know they won't find anything of value downstairs.

Sooner or later, they will make their way upstairs to her room. Now for the harder, risky part as she is no longer seventy pounds. Her body has matured and the woman in her has clearly emerged. She must release her legs and at the same time lift her tiny frame into the crawl space. Easy peasy when you are twelve, more of a challenge now. She must be stealth like, or her ceiling hideaway becomes a trap, a cage. In any event, she pushes with her right foot to get momentum. Instantly her head and upper torso shoot through the small opening, quickly right hand inside and down pushes and the rest of her emerges on the other side of the crawl space. Once up and in, she rolls her body quickly to the right and without hesitation reaches over and gently places the wooden slat back in place. She lays there catching her breath, waiting for the silence to settle in, focusing on her own breath. For now, she just lies there, her heart beating, breathing heavy.

"Settle in," she whispers to herself, "settle in and settle down, damn already need to pee." The excitement and her nerves.

She now assumes a prowler is on his way but won't normally spend much time in her room because there is clearly nothing of value, "except me, of course," she mouths to herself and lightly laughs. Now laying still, just in time to hurry up and wait, like the angels at Passover. This should not take long. Nothing worth stealing in a little girl's room. They are in, she can feel and hear it now in the connecting bathroom. Sounds like just one intruder but hard to know. The thief is probably relieved nobody home. With an empty home you can make mistakes, make noise, even turn on a light. Footsteps approaching the closet as she intentionally left the door partially open, now she hears the slow crack and creaking as it opens further. Certainly nothing of value or interest here. The housebreaker is now back in the bedroom and likely rummaging through her chest of drawers, spending a lot of time in her room. The invader is still moving around, clumsy now, clearly not worried about the noise. No way to know what he is up to or interested in. Roughly ten minutes later, he's still there. Now she can hear mumbling. The prowler is talking to himself, nothing coherent, complaining almost, pissed maybe, finding nothing to steal and hock. Now almost noisy, banging in and around her room, a laugh, did she hear a laugh then moments later a loud sharp bang, single but loud quick pound. This is no Passover angel.

Best to stay up here until her uncle is home; there's no way for her to know if intruder has come and gone.

The light through the air vent wakes her up and she opens her eyes, looking right at the attic roof not three feet from the site. She moves her head slowly to the left, realizing she fell asleep, then looking down at her legs, now realizing accidents happen. "Time to get out of here, time to change my clothes," she speaks. She lowers herself down to the closet floor, crawling in reverse. Her room is in shambles. She stands there shocked. This has never happened before, what a mess. She takes out her phone and begins to video, not sure why but makes her feel better to video the damage. She stops panning when the phone camera is aimed just after her window, middle wall over the small table, her desk. She sees it, on traditional size, 8. 5 X 11-inch printing paper a half scissor driven deep into the wall holding it like a pamphlet or poster to an outdoor post, "I KNOW WHAT YOU ARE."

Emphasis clearly on the WHAT. She tries to call Brandon but no answer. Now she does a quick scan of the room and her stuff to see what might have disappeared or is missing. She decides to text Brandon along with a picture of the cryptic message, and a short explanation of what she thinks happened.

"I am fine, and all is good, call when you can, only one thing missing from my room that I can tell, my diary." She hits send.

Chapter Seven

'It's a diary," she said yesterday, looking at me while shrugging her shoulders, hands turned and palms up. "Everything in my life fair game." Losing it hurt more than she cares to admit. The diary was her personal link to the recent past. including lots of interesting things about me, I secretly hope. Now likely gone. The photos Dan gave her are safe and secure, thrown to the floor during the destruction, now repaired and back to the panel near her bed.

I have an idea to get the diary back, assuming it still exists. My plan, if successful, would likely expose Robert Jr., as the Texas Madman. Would also expose Robert Jr., to his dad, expose the Dr, Jekyll and Mr. Hyde that he is. However, I am sensitive to the fact he just lost his wife. My plan is simple and straightforward and would make my own dad proud. It triggers another one of Ron's life accounting-isms, "when in doubt on a course of action use the straight-line method," he would say. I'm still working on the plan so haven't mentioned to the group but figured all we got to do is get an invite to Alcott's house then play it by ear and see what happens.

On my way to the school gym Wednesday early afternoon, school almost out for the summer and we have an informal basketball practice today. Informal because summer practices are not sanctioned in Ohio, but I am looking forward to the workout and the competition. I told Jimmy I choose to walk rather than ride.

"Whatever," his standard reply.

It feels good to be out walking to school again. I find myself pretending sophomore year just started, beginning of the school year not the end. I am mentally trying to make a list of everything that has happened. Organizing the events in my mind. I don't think I will put to writing. I laugh at myself, thinking of Jules's missing diary. To add to the list, Ming's let me know yesterday nothing is hidden behind the existing print of *The Thirty-Nine Steps*, nothing he can find. Remembering now as I approach school grounds, central to the story, Hannay must break the secret code. The coded notes left behind in a little black book to expose the spy ring and their dastardly plot. Fortunately for England, he did not give up and eventually broke the code and saved the world. Binky might be challenging me to think like Hannay.

"Think like Hannay," I say out loud, pretending to hear Binky say it to me just as I step up and open the door to our last practice.

Now just standing here, door open, cold air racing past me holding in its place the Cincinnati humidity and heat. Looking forward to the summer is all I am thinking, eyes closed as the air conditioning blows and cools. Jules and I both signed up for drivers training. Looking forward to that too. Then I hear a loud, long, rolling thunder, deep enough to make me hesitate, still holding the door open as I looked around.

Thick dark clouds formed wall to wall they are moving away, having passed over me a strong wind nudging them south.

"Wow didn't see that coming," I say out loud, feeling Hannay and I now in sync. I step inside, the gym door closes, and my summer officially begins.

Here we go again the three of us; Jules, Jimmy, and me at the Cincinnati Zoo and Botanical Garden, better known as the CZBG. We got a personal invitation from Alcott to have a late breakfast with the apes and go behind the scenes and meet KY, the Bonobo.

Alcott is here and waiting for us to make our way to the exhibit. Apparently, he has been coming here for years, visiting and feeding the bonobo, KY. Jimmy wants to check out the kangaroo exhibit, the first exhibit along the way and just to the left of a watering hole inside the zoo compound. Jules is in line for drinks now, and Jimmy catches me admiring Jules from afar. He and I are standing together between Jules and the kangaroos.

"You know," Jimmy says catching my gaze and teeing up the conversation, "it's obvious your kids," as Jimmy nods toward Jules then back to me, "your kids," he picks back up, "won't be able to dunk." Jules's kind of waves at us as she sees Jimmy nod, sensing conversation is likely about her.

" Let's face it, you barely clear rim now. As cute as she is, her teeny frame won't be adding any vertical lift to the family gene pool. Sometimes only the best of friends will tell you the hard truth," he continues with a cheap sigh and feigning deep sadness and regret.

Truth be told, I am not much of a dunker and vertical lift is not a part of my game. Reminiscing now about Alexandria, six foot tall and a leaper, spiker on the volleyball team. Our children would have been Jordanesque, I think to myself.

"What about the slam dunk I had against Princeton," I quickly defend.

"First," Jimmy responds, "you leaned on and pushed off their center's shoulder. Probably bought you a foot of air, even the referee was shaking his head. Only slam we saw is when you fell to the floor looking for a foul."

"Which I got and coolly sank the free throw," I remind him.

"Not saying she's not worth it, Jules that is, but maybe we should skip the baby kangaroos," he says, completely side-stepping my attempt to deflect.

I jump back in, "You recall the newspaper article following the game describing my leadership as grounding the team in every fundamental. "The writer got that right, spot on," Jimmy quickly jumps to respond.

He continues, "the grounded part." Jules now walks up hands full of goodies and sees Jimmy laughing.

"Here you go, guys," she says, divvying out cans of water to each. "What's up?" she asks." Anything I should know about?"

"Nothing really," Jimmy gets out before I can comment, "just wondering why you and Branded don't take up tennis. I hear you can play until you're ninety and it's such a well-grounded game," he says with encouraging grin, looking at both Jules and me. Jules knows something is afoot but decides to ignore and start walking so she does and as always, we take up behind and follow. Continuing our basketball banter as we gain momentum and off, we go, the three of us to Africa and beyond.

There are a couple of main streets throughout CZBG. Without any real prompting, we fell onto one joining the crowd. Numerous tight walkways lead off these streets, each walkway leading to a different animal compound. Each in its own way thickly shaded and lined in bamboo and other local plants and trees. Sunshine is literally fighting through overhead interconnected limbs and leaves to dry bottom. Before long we spot the Gorilla World sign.

"Group selfie," screams Jules and our brood swarms the sign. Ape, teenage noises, and mannerisms amazingly similar no surprise there. Only seconds pass and we soon bipedal off to the left down the dark and narrow path. Some of the bonobos have their own exhibit. We soon discover and to find them you must venture deep into Gorilla World. No problem for us. We are enjoying the various exhibits, stopping regularly to match the monkey species with teachers we know, the Colobus species and Mr. Reagan, sophomore year science teacher taking first prize. Before long we are upon the bonobos at the entrance a "drum" sign is posted outside the entrance to the exhibit. To keep in touch, the sign elaborates, bonobo tribes drum their hands, feet, and large butts against roots of trees, the base sound created carrying up to half a mile through the Congo jungle. Jimmy, wondering out loud if this is how we should signal Alcott we have arrived, his right hand extended toward a large tree, inviting Jules to give it a go. Jules, way ahead of the butt drum method, sends a text to Robert. Alcott is quick to respond, indicating we just need to venture right another fifty feet to authorized persons only sign. Take the path and he will meet us outside the fence.

"What took you so long?" he asks. "Really, a quick walk once inside the park?"

All three of us point to, look at and blame the other, Three Stooges like. Alcott just laughs, panning between the three of us.

"I understand," he says. "Come here once a month and never tire of wandering around. So here is the thing," he continues. "The staff is inside the compound with us, just not obvious. They typically stand back and down. KY is very used to me; we have seen each other almost monthly for many years. However, she was given a little medicine this morning and acting a bit drowsy. Her response time might be a little off. She is still a wild chimp, a wild animal. Move slowly as we approach and follow my lead. If she comes forward, stay still and remain calm. I have never seen her lose temper, even after all these years.

"Jimmy," he says looking right at him, "be good. There are silverback gorillas right on the other side of the tree wall so don't tempt me," Robert finishes. Jules, hand over her mouth quietly laughs. It is interesting that Robert has not brought up the Binky connection. He may be so engrossed with KY that it no longer registers. Recalling our last zoo visit, Jules and I and the bonobos long, drawn out, blank stare wondering if KY will or can remember? We don't have to wonder for long. Before we are even halfway to the monkey inside the compound it rises and turns to face us. Not four feet tall probably fifty or so pounds upright to start but quickly falling forward to long arms, long fingered hands, knuckles down and feet flat. Leaning slightly forward on all fours, head, and shoulders up as Alcott extends his hands, indicating we should slow our approach.

"The hand walking posture is a good sign," he says very lightly, "but let's give her some time to process this group." As we stand there, I look around the compound, now looking inside to out. There are a few people milling around our previous visitor's spot to the outside. Numerous large tree-like structures inside, all laid to the ground, all made to look naturally dead, around us. Bonobos love to climb, sit, and sleep in trees. As we stand there, a thought sneaks up on me; Jimmy thinks Binky, as a Folder, is inside Alcott, now likely controlling his conscience. Alcott believes Binky's essence is inside KY as the lone living chimp from Anna's original compound. All three; Binky, her conscience, and Mr. Alcott have been communing monthly for years. This triad of life appears to be working peacefully and amicably.

This thought immediately makes me think of the Ripfold I saw the last time we visited KY, the bonobo. Sure, enough, there it is, dangling or hovering for lack of a better description, behind and over KY. The Ripfold looks normal but for its size, as it is clearly smaller than most of the ones Jules and I encounter. In addition, it emits a muted luminescent glow, not the brighter light we see in most. Finally, I remember now that Jules cannot see this fold.

As I am looking it begins to move, or KY begins to move, the Ripfold apparently just along for the ride. Both now coming toward us might sound funny, but this makes me nervous. I never had a large wild animal this close before. KY kind of drags her knuckles and shuffles slowly toward us. The closer she gets the more nervous I become, sensing the same feelings in Jimmy and Jules. Robert is now crouching down to his haunches, hips and butt between his calves but not touching ground, looking smaller than the approaching bonobo. They hug, they both have their arms lightly wound around each other and now face to face. Not for long though, as Alcott falls back on his rear, laughing, releasing KY as he plops the chimp now just casually sitting next to him apparently not a care in the world. The casual nature of the scene is relaxing to me and the others, as Robert starts to lift himself, slowly stands and offers his left hand to KY. She takes it, and they turn to face us. Instinctively, all three of us begin to crouch. Robert, however, is quick to indicate it is fine to remain standing. KY begins to pull on Robert and without hesitation goes directly to Jules. She is standing between both Jimmy and me, but Robert indicates Julia should crouch down, haunch like. As she does the chimp goes right to her hair. Crouched, Jules does not look any larger than KY but it's her hair getting all the attention. It is hand tied and sitting atop her head as always. Not for long as KY pulls on an open strand and it cascades to mid- shoulder, front and back. KY is clearly intrigued, fascinated really as she begins picking through her crown while holding the thick brunette locks in her fingers. Jules is smiling and appears open and calm, letting KY have her way until KY begins to sniff, then lick, and finally mouth a large chunk of hair. Jules now is noticeably nervous. Probably wondering if KY has eaten recently, this mopping goes on for a few minutes as the chimp and Jules get better acquainted. Jimmy, Robert, and I are just watching the two of them convalesce. Finally, a Zookeeper emerges from the far left, hand signaling to Robert its time, and KY, sensing a meal with the keepers' presence, quickly breaks rank and is gone. All of us now stand quietly together single file inside the monkey compound and cage, the four of us facing and looking down at the small visitors' crowd beyond the large crevice and gathered below. A few now pointing and looking at us, probably wondering how to buy backstage tickets to meet the bonobos, up close and personal.

All four of us now standing outside KY's cage standing on the trail saying our goodbyes and Mr. Alcott thanks us for coming. He is clearly happy and openly invites us to his house for dinner this Friday evening. He wants us to meet Robert, his son, before he returns to San Antonio. I quickly accept the invitation to all but ask if we are good to bring Ming's.

"Of course, of course," he indicates. "I should have thought of that myself. You may know by now, but I put Peter in contact with Mr. Ernie Millar. A good man, I have worked with him for years. He can help Peter, your Ming's," he corrects, "with the Assembler and Combiner connectivity."

Now all of us turning and waving goodbye as we begin drifting up the trail before long, we are through the zoo and back at the car. The parking lot is now mostly full, indicating summer vacation has kicked in for many. As I open the door for Jules, I see it reflected in the side window looking no different from before, now floating overhead, my head. We have a fourth passenger along for the ride. KY's Ripfold is now following us or more accurately I think, following me.

Chapter Eight

"What happened?" he says out loud to himself. Now shaking and trying to clear his head. No one near or around that he can see. "Where the hell am I?" Now sitting straight up in his mother's car, his recently deceased mother's car. His dad wants him to ship it back to Texas with him when he goes. No recognition of the general area, Cincinnati somewhere, side road under a bridge, what he is guessing are rail tracks above. He puts his head back to rest, eyes closed now, remembering recent events in San Antonio.

"Over near the medical center," he says aloud. No one around to join the conversation, "the old monkey truck rammed into the corner pole. No recollection of what happened, nothing comes to mind, nothing at all. I had to have been driving, how else could I have been there at that time, at that moment?" he speaks.

"Remember walking up the truck back gate, gathering myself, strength returning, had trouble breathing. Looked up to see a smaller purple bicycle in the truck bed front wheel bent badly; handlebar collapsed in opposite direction."

"This can't be good," he remembers saying out loud. "This feels bad, really bad," he repeated over and over while leaning heavily on the tailgate. Now in Cincinnati with head up and sitting behind the wheel, the same feeling creeping up on him. Caught in the act again, "But caught in the act of what," he says, "driving? Where have I been? What am I doing here?"

In San Antonio, he quickly left the scene, walked home, made for long day, even longer night. Maybe nothing happened tonight, maybe just out to grab a bite, a late-night run for a Big Boy.

Blacked out again, not that unusual, it runs in the family. It's almost a weekly occurrence with dad when we were growing up. He and his mom's car parked under the bridge and up against the cubby of the curve. The engine is not on, but the keys are in the ignition. Robert starts up the car, now ready to pull out. He puts the car in reverse but with his foot on the brake.

"Let's go find a Frisch's and get that Big Boy burger," he says out loud, "get out of here and back to dad's." As he looks to pull out, he first looks to the left then behind to check for oncoming, laughing to himself. Old habits. Not a single car has come through here since he parked, but he checks anyway. "The Catholic boy in me," he mutters.

When looking behind to the rear window, he sees it on the seat, just sitting there on the back seat. A small book more like a journal, a snap journal, with a brown leather cover and a strap. Looks new, out of place. "I don't think it was there before. The last time I drove this car. Don't think its mom's either," he says to no one as he puts the gear shifter back in park. Foot still on the brake, he begins to turn and lean, right hand now reaching back.

He grabs the book, now holding it with both hands flat to his chest. This action causes an intense wave of obsession to stream toward him. Frame after frame, he now clearly sees the events of that night; compulsively stalking the girl, breaking the back window and door, calmly, coldly hunting the prey, battering her room and belongings. Finally laughing and lodging a demented notice between the wall and bladed half scissor. The other half, he now recalls, pointedly saved for her. The brutality of this vision shocks him.

"How did I get here?" he says." What am I? I'm just a normal guy. I have my own business, not a monster, polite and easy going. I even open doors for old ladies. I'm a not a savage, I'm really not a savage," Robert Jr., says, drained and weak, shoulders sloped, hands slipping from the steering wheel, head down. After a moment or two, he slowly regains his strength, anger growing in him. He knows what the problem is, he knows who is to blame.

"This is my father's virus, his virus killed mom, now it's killing me," he screams alone in his car. Now he is pounding the steering wheel, over and over, harder, and harder. Both hands echoing repentance, confession, and now intended retribution.

Lying at home in bed, I'm wondering what to do about the new addition to my shadow. KY's Ripfold. I like the way Ripfolds sound kind of like rip tide. Google indicates rip tides are often used by surfers to jump past breaking waves, like a river running out to sea. I like the way that sounds as well. In truth, I don't see it very often. KY's Ripfold. I think of it even less. I probably would forget about it all together if I didn't occasionally catch it reflected in a mirror or window.

Jules doesn't see KY's Ripfold. I modeled it for her yesterday, in jest, just having fun, to get her attention. Trying to make her look at me; twinkle toed, pinky up and butt out, just like they do on TV, she was clearly more interested in other things.

"Nothing there I would grab," she said in jest--I think or hope. So, I am back to assuming I am the only one that sees it. Logic would imply Binky made it and left it for me, but again what a leap of faith. Even in this over- the-top world of mine, that idea seems a little crazy. Jules thinks I should just grab the hitchhiking Ripfold and see what happens, jump right in. No surprise there, but I'm not comfortable with that idea right now. Ming's appears to have the warehouse computers, Assemblers and Combiners online.

Mr. Millar or Ernest, as Ming's refers to him, is way ahead in the programming field, having spent couple of decades with Girta. With Assemblers now visible to us, we need to know more before entering. Recalling Ming's previous concern about spurring or raising the attention of the Feds and others.

I'm wondering if the key to this unique Ripfold isn't locked up in the attic hidden away in one of the novels still inside Binky's box.

The trouble is which one and where. There's no way to know for now, and for now I choose to ignore it, the Ripfold that is. I need to focus on dinner at Alcott's Friday night. He wants us to meet his son. I'm not sure how to present myself and the team to Robert Jr. without setting him off. Just looking at him during the burial seemed to push him violently to invade Jules's privacy. Back to *The Thirty-Nine Steps*. I am thinking. What would Hannay do?

Maybe we could all wear sunglasses. Did Hannay ever wear sunglasses? We could be like the new Men in Black. Men in Black IV starring three teens in jeans, t-shirts, and sunglasses. Probably not the image producers are looking for the next big blockbuster. Maybe wearing sunglasses is not a bad idea. It's possible that I am responsible for spurring the Texas Madman out of Robert Jr. Sunglasses might prevent the intense eye contact that seems to have been the catalyst twice before. I need to talk to Jules and Jimmy about this idea.

"Sunglasses? No way, that's just goofy. Don't look at him," Jimmy says. It's now early Friday evening and we are driving to Alcott's house in Montgomery. I have a pair of cheap sunglasses ready and waiting. Dark clouds are overhead and it's lightly raining, so glasses are sitting in my lap.

"Keep it simple, just cough a lot and cover your face and mouth when you do. Complain about allergies, that will keep you guys from any serious eye contact," Jimmy continues. "Based on what little we know, this Jekyll and Hyde act is more a schizo thing with Robert Jr. It must come and go or Robert Sr. would be more aware of the problem. He is clearly in the dark about his son. Jr. will likely be more focused on Jules anyway, like he was at the burial," Jimmy points out.

"Someone should remind the perv she is only sixteen while he is clearly over thirty," Jimmy quickly adds.

"It's hard to argue with that," Jules adds.

"And Jules," Jimmy continues, not ready to let her off the hook, "you need to be alert enough to jump in and distract Mr. Hyde if he focuses in on Branded," Jimmy instructs.

"Yes sir," she salutes and responds.

"Same goes for you Jimmy," I say jumping in. "Remember, part of our mission here is to look for the diary. Jules needs a chance to try and find her journal."

"What's the plan?" asks Jules.

"I figure early on we just ask Sr. for a tour of his beautiful house, during which we find out where Robert Jr. is staying. Then it's up to you," I say, turning to the back seat and looking at Jules, this time with my cool rays on. This cracks her up as Jimmy and me join in and the laughter grows.

Soon thereafter Google indicates we have arrived. The house is not quite what I expected, not the large dark Tudor mansion I envisioned. Nice two-story open, red brick, big windows, lots of trees and shrubs, with semi-circle drive pathway running along the entire front of house. Yard like things dispersed throughout: fountain, small gnomes, and inviting ornate table hidden in a corner alcove. Looking quite friendly, and very well-kept. As we pull in, I look quickly at both Jimmy and Jules.

"Look guys one more thing, nothing risky tonight, okay? If all we do is spend time with the Alcott's and get to know them a little better, that's a win," I say as we begin to pile out of the car.

Robert Sr. comes out to greet us, coming down the walk leading from the front door.

"Welcome guys," he says as all three of us emerge from the vehicle and now up and out returning the hellos. "I understand Ming's cannot join us, sorry to hear," he says to Jimmy more directly as the two of them now shake hands. Jules and I circle around the vehicle to join the greeting. It's no longer a steady rain but there are ominous clouds hovering directly overhead. Light drizzle begins to fall.

"Well typically I'd start the tour from the outside, but it's likely to turn into a sprint. It's supposed to rain heavy; probably best we head inside," he says, looking skyward. Robert now holds open the front door, Jules leading the way.

One by one we all step into the foyer of the house. The first thing that strikes me is a giant picture window along the back wall. The entrance area with sitting room is to the left, a stairway somewhat straight ahead and master bedroom to the right. As we venture further inside, we pass a door to the right with another stairway, this time leading down. We notice off to the left the kitchen area. The view from the window kind of draws everyone into the large living room straight ahead. The four of us are now gathered there. The entire back wall consists of three giant floor-to-ceiling windowpanes looking directly into numerous tree-top canopies, giving the home a unique treehouse like feel. As we get acclimated, the wind and rain begin to hit hard. This adds to the effect and the three of us are somewhat speechless.

Robert breaks the silence. "When people visit, we always start and end the home tour right here. Everyone is drawn to the windows. Really in a way you just saw the entire house," he says.

The stairway at the entrance leads upstairs, office, guest bedroom, and workout area. Robert Jr. has the whole floor to himself. The master bedroom is to the immediate right as we entered. The stairway with the door leads," as he leans and points to the right, "to a downstairs apartment. We built it out for my wife when she fell sick, I will likely close it off now while we look to remodel. That large double door you see in the hallway here to the right," Robert now turned and pointing in the other direction, "is an elevator covering all three floors. Really a necessity rather than luxury when you have loved one confined to a wheelchair." As he says this, we all are moving in that direction now past the elevator and into the large kitchen and dining area. Maybe the largest residential kitchen area I have ever seen. Between the multiple appliance line-up, numerous sinks, enormous middle island, and family table. Actually, family tables; one large enough for at least twelve people and another more breakfast nook oriented in a far corner seating three or four. The smaller one adjacent to a see-through fireplace bridging the kitchen to the room with a view. Finally, immediately off the kitchen is a covered screened-in outdoor area. Looking like an actual tree house complete with rain, wind, banging tree limbs and foliage. Robert gives us a chance to take it all in.

"This is my pride and joy," he says as he spreads his arms out and pans the kitchen. "I am an amateur chef and spend much of my time and energy here, cooking and creating. Having said that, I very creatively called in for pizza delivery tonight," as he points toward the kitchen table pre-loaded with three large pies. "Sorry, but Robert Jr. is out tonight, last-minute business since he is leaving early tomorrow. He's headed back here now and hopefully arrives before we finish. I promise, however, to cook a proper feast for all of you soon. Our family has always used Sunday dinners to gather, catch up, tell stories, play games, laugh, argue, and even fight. Good for the soul, I think. We've culled Sunday dinner activities back a bit the last few years as my wife struggled, but I would love to have a good reason to gear them back up," he finishes as he is looking around to the three of us.

"So, let's not wait for Robert Jr. Pizza in front of you getting cold," he says. "What would everyone like to drink?" he asks now, drifting down a short hallway apparently leading to the garage and outdoor fridge. We all begin to shout orders when Jules decides to excuse herself, at least to us. Hunting for the ladies, room, and other things, she whispers. Jimmy and I quickly understood and head directly behind Sr. to help carry drinks and distract.

Jules wastes no time and heads straight upstairs, assuming there must be a toilet up there somewhere, along, of course, with Jr.'s bedroom and things. She quickly finds both the office and bedroom connected by common bathroom. She gets down to searching through his belongings, open and mostly packed suitcase on the bed, so she starts there. Finding nothing, she straightens up and is about to turn to the bed side chest when she hears someone clear their throat. Now looking up, Robert Jr. is standing in the doorway to his room.

"Hi," he says, "have me met before, do I know you?"

"Hi, no we have not met my name is Julia. I am here with Brandon and Jimmy to have dinner with you and your father," she says.

"Find what you were looking for?" he asks calmly but with some authority.

"Well… I was going to feign need for a bathroom but that seems awfully silly now."

"You think?" Robert's quick reply.

"Well," Jules begins again, never one to beat around the bush. "To be totally honest I am looking for my diary. Robert, who had been leaning against the jamb of the door frame, quickly straightens up, posture now very different from before.

Without hesitation, he enters the room to an immediate right, crouches down, opens the drawer to a built-in part of a white chest, reaches in, and removes a plastic bag.

He walks up to Julia and hands it out to her.

"Is this it?" he asks.

Julia, just staring at it, recognizes her journal but is not able to move yet. She wants to reach and grab it, wondering why or how this could be so easy. Also knowing this is bad timing, she starts to tear up. She knows this is hers, this is her diary, her life. She can't take her eyes off it; her tears are not alone. Robert is also moved.

"I did not touch it other than to put in this bag," he says with some difficulty. "I do not know where it came from, do not know what is inside. It was in my mom's car. It is obviously yours. Please take it away from here." He is visibly moved and not sure what else to say. They stand there for a bit. Then Julia opens the bag and removes her book, hands Jr. the empty bag, slides the slim leather journal into her back jean pocket, and leaves the room.

The rest of the evening is uneventful until we leave. Jules comes back to join the conversation. She apologizes for taking so long, kind of shrugging her shoulders in explanation. Robert Sr., having raised a daughter, seems to understand and the conversation continues undisturbed. He is giving us more history about Girta. I am fascinated and taking it all in. Robert Jr. shows up as we finish.

We do introductions and Jr. apologizes for his tardiness. He looks quite normal, if distracted. No Texas Madman in sight. Jimmy keeps him engaged in small talk and presumably out of my site line. At one point soon thereafter, Jimmy reminds us he needs to get the car back. His mom has errands to run. The four of us now stand at the front door. Jules, Jimmy, myself, and Robert Sr., Jr having excused himself and gone upstairs.

Trailing the end of the conversation, Robert makes an appeal for group to meet regularly. He would be happy to host. Bragging with a large smile, "just one meal and you will be hooked." Sounds pretty good to both Jimmy and me. Jules is mostly silent.

Now the three of us are back in the car and headed to Jules's house and almost immediately she pulled out her diary, thrusting her prize between the car seats for both of us to see. Without hesitation, she begins to describe the encounter with Robert Jr.; his standing in the bedroom doorway, the direct request for her diary, and then the weird exchange thereafter, Jules adding, "he clearly had no clue, he did not know where it came from, did not know why he had it, and I believe him," she finishes.

Once again, I am struck by her attitude, getting right to the point, cutting right to the chase, the Ripfold girl, the jump right in girl, I fondly recall to myself, now smiling. Inwardly feeling proud and happy to be her friend.

We are about ten minutes out and listening to Jules when I realize there is a problem, "Guys," I scream, "Jimmy, turn around," I say loudly. "My phone, I left my phone at Alcott's, sorry Jules, for the interruption. It's probably sitting on the kitchen table. I think I may have accidentally threw a napkin over it when Jr. came in the room."

I have knocked and rung bell couple of times, no answer, no response, but we know they are home. Jimmy is getting impatient, knowing his mom will not be happy if he is not home soon, so try the door and it is unlocked. I could just run in, grab my phone, and run out, thinking to myself I know where the phone is likely sitting. I look over at Jimmy and his body language indicates we need to hurry so, thinking screw it, I open the door and step in.

Immediately, I hear strange noises, no doubt coming from the kitchen. They are muted, but strong and loud, growing louder and now more like kicking or banging. Then I hear it, I know that voice, the Texas Madman I now hear it loud and clear, "you killed our family, you killed mom, you killed our family, you killed mom," over and over he is saying with force and hatred. Moving quickly to the kitchen, I now see what is happening. Jr. has his dad pinned to the family table, using his large size to hold his body steady with one knee, both his large hands firmly around Sr's neck. His dad is trying to resist but even in the short time I am there his resistance is clearly fading. Robert does not have the strength to move him, not even a bit and life almost out of him. I know Jr. is just too big for me to grab, so I barrel toward him to tackle him, hopefully knocking him off and away from his dad. It might be too late. His dad is almost flopping now.

I'm about halfway to Jr. and gaining speed, he looks up and sees me. No doubt now it is clearly the Madman. I see that look in his eye, not one you could ever forget. Just before impact, he shifts his knee off his dad and toward me too late for me to slow or change direction. His knee and my stomach both collide, sending me hard against the smaller table and bashed against the wall. Breath is totally knocked out of me, and pain is shooting through my abdomen and side. Quickly, almost cat like, Jr. is off Robert and onto me now, his girth on my chest and hands around my neck. No resistance from me. I can't breathe. Stunned from the knee, table slam and now Jr.'s firm, menacing grip, I see Robert Sr. start to stir. Jr. the madman now screaming, "two for one, two for one, the Father of Lies and young Satan himself, Father of Lies and young Satan himself, two for one, two for one," he screams with both terror and pleasure in his voice. Both my hands are around his lower arms but there is little resistance as I still can't breathe. His powerful grip is around my throat now, thumbs like daggers above my larynx. At this rate I won't last long. Weirdly enough I am thinking very clearly, my mind not yet affected. I can't really do much with my body, but my mind is working.

Robert Sr., now up and stumbling, trying to help me, falls on top of his son, but he is just kind of hanging there, almost like resting on Jr's., back. He has no strength and. he's still trying to get his own breath. I must be turning blue because I see Sr.'s face looking right at me with a new terror in his eyes. He can sense I am losing; I can sense me losing, death probably imminent. Robert Jr. is now getting stronger, and he has no need to throw off his dad, his dad cannot budge him. I feel my head start to spin. It must be lack of oxygen, blood flow. I understand now I don't have much time left, then out of nowhere, well actually out of Robert Sr., a shadow emerges. Not slowly but with speed and intent. I remember Findlay market and the shadow that hit me knocked me hard into the Ripfold.

Without hesitation the shadow slams into Jr., I can almost feel the vibration of its entrance through his hands, which are still firmly around my neck. The grip slackens just a bit, Jr. noticeably confused; his hands haven't moved but his thumbs are no longer hard against my breathing tube, a hint of oxygen sneaks in, my brain is still clear, my body limp. Robert Sr is still a lean-to against Jr's. back. Then slowly a dark thick shadow, not wispy like before, emerges from Jr's underbelly. It is crawling slowly out of him and up my abdomen, much thicker, heavier more substantive than before. Now the larger ray-like creature has totally emerged from

Robert Jr. and ominously works its way up my torso, both of us staring at it wide-eyed, nothing else to be done. It is moving slowly but deliberately with intent.

"Binky," my brain manages to utter as it is now over my chest and approaching my neck. This causes Jr. to release his grip, not wanting anything to do with this creature. As it is about to cover and consume my face, the ray turns. It turns to the right, toward my shoulder. It turns to the Ripfold, KYs Ripfold is now clearly visible to me. Jr., still fixated on its movement, can't see it. Before long the tentacles of the creeping slurry and the fold have touched and Bang, the shadow and the Texas Madman gone, weirdly instantly the Ripfold is brighter as if glowing.

Robert Sr. falls to the floor spread eagle. Robert Jr. rolls off me, also falling to the floor, imitating his dad. I have already joined them, having been here for a while. My head is slightly propped by one of the table legs. I can see each of the Alcott's on the floor and to the far right leaning against the wall not ten feet away, I see a light. My phone lit up; someone has been texting me. Not two seconds later Jimmy and Jules come bursting into the kitchen. None of us moved even the slightest muscle. The two of them look in disbelief, wondering, like me, what just happened.

The three of us are back in the parked car and settling in. My phone lights up. "A text from Ming's," I say out loud to all. He indicates Assembler computers are quite active tonight. The Compiler in Columbus is also busy, but he has no idea what happened or what this means, I pass on to everyone.

"Not sure what happened back there either," Jimmy chimes in, flipping his head with quick motion toward the house since Jules and I came in late. "But for some reason it feels like big a win, another victory for the three amigos? Am I right, tell me I am right," Jimmy pleads.

I hesitate but then respond, "Yes, my gut tells me you are right. Not only did Jules recover her diary, but I think the Texas Madman may now be gone, maybe forever." As I say this, I look to the sideview mirror looking for KYs Ripfold I don't see anything, but I know she is there.

"Robert Jr. I think probably back to normal his old self and free will restored, Katherine, Cat and the entire Girta clan is now probably safe from retribution," I conclude. Not sure yet what to think about Robert Sr., best to keep that to myself and leave it for another day.

Jimmy, visibly feeling good about our success and ready to rock and roll, says, "I noticed Jules," quickly shifting gears back to the moment, "when you were helping Jr. to his feet maybe a little soft spot, little extra lift of kindness. Does this mean you are a Miami Vice type girl," he openly wonders while looking behind at her, then to me and now stroking his own newly sprouted stubble. Jimmy has been unshaven since semester's end. Before Jules can respond he jumps back in.

"Of course, there is always the more mature, even debonair George Clooney look," now thrusting his own bearded chin out for all to see, fisted hand firmly underneath for proper effect and support, "Clooney," I say in mock confusion "more like Snoop Dog, don't you think Jules?"

"Guys, guys," she indicates, now taking charge of the conversation. "Give a girl her due," waiting patiently for us to turn and look now sporting her best southern belle imitation, the good book sitting on her lap, hands on top neatly folded in devotion. "Truth be told this little lady…is more of a Patrick Stewart kind of gal," she adds with a not so muffled giggle.

Simultaneously, Jimmy and I both reach up and grab large locks of our own hair. "Say what?" we both scream together Jimmy then quick to add, "She's your girlfriend." Silence, then all three of us burst into loud and uncontrollable laughter in stitches, stomping our feet and having a good time.

Finally, many minutes later, Jimmy is settled enough to drive and now in reverse pulling away from the Alcott' home. The rain has

stopped, clouds have parted, sun is out but setting, laughter
dissolved into the rearview the three of us now onward as we gain
momentum and back on the road again.

That same night an older couple is at the Findlay Market, rain having stopped. are out for a short walk before dark. Together now, holding hands, strolling the Essen Strasse when out of nowhere a bolt or flash.

"Wow, that was close," the gentleman says.

"Summer lightning," his wife believes.

"Lightning is just end result of two equal but opposite reactions," the old man replies.

The couple notice hair on the back of their necks and stand.

"That's different," the old man says to no one in particular, but each now rubbing their own neck both unconsciously, picking up the pace, all eyes nervously combing the area.

Ready for more? Read on for a sneak peek into the next book,

Ripfolds II.

RIPFOLDS II
MAGICAL SUMMER

Chapter One,
Part One

Something wicked alone laying naked in the grass knows where he is, has been here before, just not recently. The sun is well beyond setting, but it's not yet completely dark. An elderly couple has just passed through. He scampers quickly to side of the building, A cocky young buck heading up the walkway in his direction has something he wants, clothing. Looking around, he sees two folded metallic chairs leaning against the wall just to the right of where he is standing. The restaurant is no longer serving, the patio probably getting ready to close. He reaches over and grabs the first folded chair with both hands. Heavy, solid it needs to be, strong winds often blow through the Findlay Market. The kid now approaching, Wicked quickly flips the munition to legs up, holding each firmly, takes one naked step forward, swinging the chair with great force, almost falls over as he swings. He loses his balance but settles in, standing over the punk chair square to the target victim down, nose shattered, clearly broken, body now flopping like a headless market fish.

"Bingo," he says out loud, "you will thank me when you get older. A broken nose adds character," he says, now looking down at him, breathing heavily, voice and body shaking. "Women like character." He steps aside and kicks the boy hard in the head, just to make sure he out and now drags him feet first behind the building.

"I hate these things," he complains to no one in particular, shaking his right foot. "Damn flip flops." Now clumsily making his way up the market pathway, the boy's clothing a bit loose, baggy even, probably fashionable.

He sees a reflection in the shop window, nervously turns to see who is following him, no one there then he remembers." Crap," he says out loud. "I just can't get used to how I look… some old white guy. bet I am at least thirty," he says with anger and disgust. Without hesitation and now with sharp intent, he turns out of the Findlay, right on Race Street and into the belly of Over-the-Rhine, a popular troubled area of downtown Cincinnati. Leaving the market behind, Jeeves knows where he is; even better, knows where he is going.

Ming's is on his way back from Columbus. It's the wee hours of the morning. He stopped to purchase a strobe light on the way yesterday, what is now yesterday, the kind they use in construction. That is all he really needs. He knows where the back door to the Combiner is located, the strobe to help him see it quickly. He needs to enter the machine before anyone from the Infectious Disease Institute sees him or the strobe. Either of these will draw the ire of building security. Something unusual happened with the Combiner last week, unusual enough for him to come to Columbus to check it out. All told, the visit went well, computer still, "as is" he says inside the car. "Just as dad and I built it, still programmed to work in conjunction with the Assembler to attract and destroy the rogue virus, the virus and everything a part of it."

He adds now with concerned emphasis but now confident he can readily hook the office machines and Combiner together, allowing he and Earnest to monitor, track, and influence activities. With the help of Earnest, the systems at the warehouse are now up and running.

"Overall, a good day's work," he says out loud to himself as he pulls up to his warehouse home. He is parked and walking up to the front door. He feels a chilled wind, unusual for June, something different, something new in the air. Probably just his imagination.

"Nothing new or different ever happens around here," he says to only the door. Then immediately he laughs out loud as he realizes where he is and what he said.

"That felt good," he says to himself, now unlocking the main entrance, "I need to laugh more often."

"Damn," is all he can say as he opens the door and steps inside. Like a cyclone unleashed, he can almost feel the rage coming off the damage. The place is in shambles. He is stunned as he dares to venture deeper into his home. He stops, looks around. Whoever did this might still be inside. He looks for something to swing, something hard and long. No movement or sounds to be heard, deathly quiet, but he can see a light coming from the back. The door must be open the porch light is shining through.

"Well, we know how they got in," he says softly and out loud, "and out," gaining confidence now he is alone. Now believing the raider long gone, he walks to the back and firmly closes the bent-up door and notices a light projected to the floor highlighting an uninvited crowbar. He spends about thirty minutes combing the destruction with the jimmy firmly in hand.

It seems the only area untouched is his small, makeshift bedroom. He sits down to the side of the bed in disgust." Now what?" Ming's says out loud to himself. Then noticing on the side table next to the bed small piece of paper, handwritten note: "more to come see you soon, Jeeves."

The four of us together again at Ming's Chinese Street Food Diner, Jules, Jimmy, Ming's, and me. Diane is here as well but waiting on other tables. She knows we aren't going anywhere anytime soon. I have described to Ming's the violence, struggle, and Ripfold jump at Alcott's home, having already covered it with Jules and Jimmy. Ming's in turn just finished updating the group on the damage to the warehouse, his home now trashed. The team is a little perplexed at what happened and what to do next when Jimmy jumps in.

"What, you guys weren't listening when we covered this before? It's obvious, at least to me, what happened; Binky inside Robert Sr. saw the Texas Madman about to take out Branded here," Jimmy said, looking directly at me. "You just said you felt moments from death. Her only recourse to leave Robert Sr., which in and of itself raises an issue for another time, another discussion. Her essence then jumps into Jr. Once inside she had to take over Sean quickly or her only son, Branded again is toast, she then drags all three of them to KY's Ripfold or everyone doomed. Sean's now likely back to running some little shop somewhere in his own world with Binky as his guiding light. Finally, Branded, you of all people are forgetting Ms. Spragen, you were her class pet, "for every action there is an equal and opposite reaction."

"Assemblers took in Binky, Sean, and his essence, the Compiler as you call it Ming's, then spit out the Findlay Crawler, equal and opposite side of the equation. Jeeves and whomever he is inside, now roaming our world freely and with abandon. We have no clue what he looks like. He is free from any identity, free to do whatever he wants, including trashing our headquarters, the little scum bag," Jimmy concludes.

"Jimmy, you have a colorful way of putting things," Ming's indicates. "To add to the color, Alcott has already offered his basement home to rebuild the network. He has even offered me the apartment side of the living area and he was quick to add I could have free run of the entire downstairs."

"Well so much for waiting to discuss the elephant in the room," Jimmy says, jumping back in. "If I am correct about Binky then she is no longer inside Alcott. Robert Sr., now back to who he was before, a bit rusty perhaps but his old nasty self. Binky is no longer there to control the dark side you previously despised," Jimmy says, now looking directly at Ming's.

Jules patiently listens to the conversation, then steps in. "Everything happens for a reason," she points out, changing the tone of the conversation and slowly panning to all three of us. "We need Mr. Alcott, we need each other. All we need to do now is find Jeeves and free him from the Crawler. They just want their lives back, free of each other and free again to make their own decisions. Seems simple enough," she ends.

Diane is now up to the table, that motherly patient look at each of us, and calms settles in amongst the group.

"Well, what will it be tonight? she inquires, "Something new, different, and exciting or more of the same?" Before she can even move her pen, we all loudly demand, unrehearsed, and in unison, "same!"

TO BE CONTINUED…

ripfolds

Bob was born and raised in Cincinnati, Ohio. He put himself through college in West Virginia, playing basketball and working at several odd jobs, including midnight attendant in the emergency room of the local hospital.

It was working in the emergency room that convinced Bob to forego his pre-med degree and attend law school. He decided to attend law school in a warmer climate, choosing St. Mary's University in San Antonio, Texas. As a second-year law student, Bob applied for a legal clerk's position with a small but growing San Antonio-based medical company and his career began.

Bob is an experienced commercial real estate professional and attorney, licensed in Texas, and college professor at the University of Texas-San Antonio. He still lives in San Antonio some thirty years later, hitting the trails daily with his dog and daily companion, Curtis. Curtis, however, has recently passed. Several years of wildlife photos, "Cruising with Curtis" can be seen on the web site; www.ripfolds.com. Most of these pictures were taken while Bob and Curtis were walking together in and around the Cibolo Creek near the family homestead in South Texas.

In early 2005 a Cincinnati, Ohio based technology company was engaged by Department of Defense to develop a viral based vaccine to help treat post-traumatic stress disorder and other divergent issues. A computer-generated virus was created and driven by the emotion of the host to attack memory. The virus went AWOL, mutated, spread outside of the intended scope and outside the company. All members of the science team were infected, all offspring of the science team thought to be carriers. Two of these progenies: Brandon Fair, only son of the company's chief scientist and Julia Childs are infected but also very gifted.

This story is about three young teenagers; two with unique gifts to travel in time and one just unique. Brandon, Jules, and Jimmy learning early in life to think for themselves and care for each other.

"Ripfolds are like cuts or wounds in the sky," Brandon says to Jimmy. "Jules and I see the Ripfolds and know what they represent. When either Jules or I grab a fold, we are thrown into another place and time, inside another person. Once inside we are programmed to connect the person's memory to the lost moment and overcome the effects of the virus. If we don't connect the memory the Ripfold will close and vanish. The virus is successful, and time is changed."

9 780984 534692